THE
SACRED
SUMMER

BY CATRINA ROSE

◆ FriesenPress

Suite 300 - 990 Fort St
Victoria, BC, V8V 3K2
Canada

www.friesenpress.com

ISBN
978-1-03-910190-6 (Hardcover)
978-1-03-910189-0 (Paperback)
978-1-03-910191-3 (eBook)

Young Adult Fiction, Fantasy, Contemporary

Distributed to the trade by The Ingram Book Company

*To my children, parents, siblings, nieces,
nephews, and to the love of my life.
You inspired this story.*

I love you all, dearly.

xo

PART ONE

MISSING

Guard well thy Cause from your descendants
ere they receive their powers.
From the moment of Knowledge, Descendants of the Tree
shall be compelled by the tasks set before you.

AUGUST 2008

Abby

They'd driven for hours in silence. Abby tried to imagine how her new life would be.

"Why wasn't Aunt Lacey's son at her funeral?" Jack suddenly asked. Abby wondered too.

"Probably because she wasn't much of a mother," said her stepfather. Abby winced. Her stepfather had little consideration for her mother's feelings. Predictably, they began arguing.

Abby tuned them out. As she watched the road signs and hillsides glide by, she thought about how Aunt Lacey abandoned her son. *Just like my dad abandoned me.* Her thoughts were interrupted by her stepfather's angry whisper.

"You said so yourself that she was a witch," he said. "A crazy, gallivanting witch."

"That is not what I said, Michael. She is not a witch. And please don't speak as if she's dead," her mother calmly replied.

"We went to her funeral two weeks ago, Julea," Michael responded contemptuously.

"She has disappeared. No one knows for sure she is dead," Julea replied and arched her eyebrows.

"She's been gone for two years," Michael continued. "We are moving into her house today."

"Yes. We are." Julea's voice hardened.

"I'm just saying, you might have to eventually accept that she's gone," Michael placated.

It was true. Abby's mother had inherited the family house and riverside property. Today the Sider-Bagwell family would begin their new life on the Sider Farm.

At long last, the Sider-Bagwells pulled off the highway into Beaverdell. They stopped to buy enough groceries to get them through a few days of unpacking. It was still an hour drive to the farm and this was the closest convenience store to them.

Beaverdell had one gas station, one general store, and three pubs. Abby counted them as they drove down what was clearly the main street of the town – and the highway through it. As they neared what looked like the last houses before everything turned to trees again, Michael turned right at her mother's direction. They rounded the corner and saw a crowd of adults and children sitting on a bridge deck covered with lawn chairs. One fellow puffed on a pipe. A tall, blonde boy looked like he was about to dive into the river.

At the sight of their car, the small mob began standing up and gathering themselves, their chairs, and their coolers to each side of the bridge deck. Children scrambled down the slopes to move out of the way, their heads poking up out of the grass to peer at the strangers. A burly, bearded man gestured "be my guest" with a low arm wave, signaling for them to pass through.

Michael rolled down his window and pulled up slowly to the friendly-looking fellow.

"Hi there," he said. "Beautiful day, isn't it? The wife and I are just heading out to the Sider Farm."

The burly fellow scrunched his eyebrows and ducked his head to look in the back seat at Abby and Jack. His eyes passed over them swiftly before turning to settle on Abby's mother.

"Well, hello there pretty thing," he said gruffly.

"Hello Angus," Julea said with a smile. "I'm back."

Angus let out a loud whoop and skipped around the car as Julea climbed out. He caught her up in his arms and squeezed her hard. "I told you you'd come back! But I didn't wait for you. That's my wife coming over now. And those are my kids," he pointed to five scruffy kids, now standing back on the bridge deck, staring curiously at Abby and Jack. "Cash, Cathryn, Kenny, and Olivia. Except for the dark-haired one," Angus said softly. "That's our mutual nephew, Travis."

Abby watched as her mother's eyes fell on the dark boy. She looked stunned. Abby climbed out of the car intending to introduce herself to the cousin she'd never met. He was Aunt Lacey's boy. His father was raising him. Seeming offended by all the attention, Travis melted out of the crowd and down the bank towards the river.

"I'll send him over with Frank once you're settled in," Angus promised.

Their car sat in the middle of the bridge but no one seemed to be concerned. Julea made introductions.

"Michael, this is Angus McAllister," she said. "Angus, this is my husband, Michael Bagwell." She turned to her husband. "Lacey and I spent whole summers running wild with Angus and his brother, Frank. When I grew older and left the farm, Angus told me I'd be back."

"And here you are," Angus nodded solemnly, the reason for her return acknowledged in the air between his words.

Michael gladly accepted a beer and lapsed easily into friendly conversation. Abby assessed the scraggly blonde brood known as Angus' offspring.

She noticed the oldest boy, Cash, right away. He was taller than her and looked a bit older. He was looking at her too. She smiled and turned away. "Jack. Go say hi to them or something," she nudged her brother attempting to hide her embarrassment.

"Okay," he replied. He walked over to the boy who looked closest to his age. "Are you swimming in the river?" he asked.

"Yeah, do you wanna check it out?" replied the boy.

"Kenny, he might get his clothes dirty," his older sister, Cathryn, warned.

"It's okay," said Jack. "My mom won't care." Jack, Kenny, Cathryn, and the youngest sibling, Olivia, began to half-climb half-slide down the embankment towards the river. Abby felt Cash looking at her again. This time she met his eyes. A mini thrill surged through her.

"Do you want to go for a swim?" he asked.

"Umm, no thanks. I'm not a very good swimmer," she admitted.

"Well, if you change your mind, I'm a great swimmer, and I could always save you if you drown." Cash winked at her roguishly. He took two steps and dove backwards over the edge of the bridge. Abby's heart pounded as water splashed at her feet. *Stupid fear of water!* she scolded herself.

***

The house was large and sprawling, with a porch that encircled it. Vines and flowers grew against it. Squirrels skittered across the railings as the car pulled up. Michael had predicted the house would be in shambles ––dusty and falling apart from two years of abandonment. But Julea had said, "It won't be so bad." And it wasn't. In fact, it was quite spotless.

"Whoa. I wonder who's been keeping up the house all this time," said Michael.

"Probably some little dust pixies," Julea teased, looking at her children. "Remember what I told you. This place is magical." She looked around at the flowers and sighed with pleasure. "Home sweet home."

"Okay Mom," Abby rolled her eyes, but couldn't help smiling. "Actually, it looks pretty cool here," she said, thinking of Cash McAllister. "And I can't wait to see my room!" She bounded up the porch steps with Jack close behind. Julea unlocked the door to let them inside while Michael wandered around the house in search of the workshop he'd been promised.

Jack

Abby and Jack's rooms were identical. They faced each other from opposing sides of the attic. Each of them had a large bay window they could open wide and sit in with their feet resting on the slanting roof.

The rooms were immaculately clean. They looked as though they'd been arranged and waiting for Abby and Jack specifically.

Jack's room was swathed in deep blues and greens with antique armoires and bedside tables with legs on them that made them look as though they could get up and walk away.

He crossed over to Abby's room. She was surrounded by frilly, lavender velvet curtains. Her bedspread and a throw blanket that lay across a chair in the corner matched the curtains. Her armoire and bedside tables were the same as his. She stood at her window, looking down.

"This place is creepy," said Abby when Jack walked up behind her. She stared down at a blood-red rose that lay across the windowpane. "How do you suppose that got there?"

"I don't know," Jack replied blandly. "Maybe it was Mom," he suggested.

"Mom hasn't been upstairs," Abby replied. She shrugged. "Maybe it was a blood-red rose fairy," she chuckled nervously.

"You're as strange as Mom is," Jack replied.

Abby

The following day, Abby and Jack decided to explore the property together. Behind the house was a barn, a wood shed, and Michael's workshop. The grassy yard spread out against a backdrop of apple orchards, forest, and mountains.

They went in search of the river. Their mother told them it was the same water Jack swam in with the McAllisters. What luck that it ran right through their property.

Jack ran ahead of Abby, down the path and through the trees in the direction their mother had indicated. "You can't miss it," she'd said.

The path wound around a patch of pine trees on the left and the apple orchard on the right. Abby saw the tree before she saw the river. It loomed in the background at the end of a long row of apple trees, much bigger than the rest. As she neared it, she saw its branches waving in the breeze in such a way that it appeared to be beckoning to her. She felt like she was under a tree spell. Giggling at her own weirdness, she turned the path heading towards the rushing hiss of water.

A noise from behind stopped her. Suspecting that Jack was trying to scare her, Abby whirled around to catch him. Instead, she was surprised to see a big, fat, golden apple rolling down the slope towards her. It stopped at her feet.

Abby smiled. *This is so meant to be.* She picked up the apple, gave it a light rub knowing that no Sider-grown fruit would ever contain pesticides, and bit into the juiciest, most delicious apple she'd ever tasted in her life. Flavour burst through her mouth. Her body hummed. Her taste buds rejoiced. She imagined she could hear the tree sigh with pleasure as she enjoyed its scrumptious bounty.

Okay, Abs, get a hold of yourself. It's just an apple, she thought with amusement. But she gladly took another bite before heading towards the river to find her brother.

Jack

Jack imagined several scenarios that might occur when he planted his shoes and shirt beside the river. He climbed up into the foliage of a tree where he could secretly watch his sister's reaction. He thought she might know he was playing a joke on her and tell him to knock it off. She hated it when he jumped out from a hiding spot and scared her.

If she believed the trick, she might get hysterical and start screaming his name or calling for help. She might go running back to the house to tell Mom. Jack knew he'd have to jump down and stop her before she alarmed the Mom-inator. Julea would not be impressed by this kind of prank.

He braced himself for quick descent when Abby came around the corner chewing on an apple and saw his shoes.

"Jack?" she said uncertainly. Jack stayed very still.

Abby looked around the small clearing, eyeing the bushes suspiciously. She scanned the surface of the water for a few seconds. "Jack?" she said again, louder.

Jack remained silent. He could see that his sister was about to freak. He held back the rumble of laughter building in his chest. Jack expected her to run towards the house. He was totally unprepared for Abby's next move.

She dropped the apple and braced her legs as though she were going to dive into the water.

"NO!" Jack yelled as he hurled his body from the tree, tackling Abby to the ground.

"What are you doing?" yelled Jack, struggling to climb off of her. "I didn't think you'd dive into the water. Since when do YOU dive into the water?"

Abby appeared stunned. "I…I don't know what I was thinking," she stammered.

"What were you going to do once you were in there? You can't even swim. We'd both be dead," he scolded angrily. Seeing his sister preparing to dive into the swift-moving river had scared the heck out of him.

Abby seemed to gather herself. "Well, you shouldn't play tricks like that, Jack," she snapped at him. "I thought you were drowning. Mom would be so mad if I told her."

"Please don't tell Mom," said Jack as his heart rate slowed to a more natural pace. "I'm sorry."

Abby didn't answer him. She scooted up the bank to rest under a tree and stared at the river.

Jack wanted to go back to the house and see what treasures were to be found in the huge old barn. But he felt nervous about his sister almost jumping in the river. He knew it was very unlikely but he couldn't bring himself to leave her after that near-miss. He sat down and rooted around in the grass for flat rocks.

"I already like it here," said Abby after a few moments. Jack knew what she meant. He too was already feeling attached to the place and they'd just moved in the day before. All misgivings about leaving his friends behind had vanished.

"Do you think Aunt Lacey will come back and want her house?" he asked Abby, as he skipped a rock on the water.

"I already asked Mom about that," she replied. "She said Aunt Lacey didn't really live here before anyway. She lived with Travis and Frank on the McAllister lands. Mom promised that this is our home now."

"Dad thinks Aunt Lacey is dead."

"Yeah. But Mom says she's not dead," said Abby. "She says she would know if her sister was dead. Mom's usually right."

"Yeah," said Jack. "But we did go to her funeral. Mom could be wishful thinking because she doesn't want to believe her sister is dead."

Abby nodded her head and shrugged. "I'm not going to tell Mom about you pretending to drown because it would remind her of losing Aunt Lacey. But please don't ever do it again."

"Believe me, I won't," assured Jack. "I'm too scared you'll jump in after me and kill yourself."

Abby smiled. "Wanna go back? I want to pick some apples on the way for Mom," she said.

"Yuck," said Jack, as he picked up his shirt and shoes. "I hate apples."

Abby

She walked into the kitchen with her shirt full of apples and found her mom talking to herself while she prepared lunch. Abby felt sad for her mom. *What would it feel like if Jack died?* She couldn't imagine.

"Guess what, Mama," she said as she dumped her load onto the sturdy wooden table. She scooped quickly to catch them, as apples rolled in all directions. Abby wanted to tell her mom about a wolf she'd seen across the river when she and Jack were preparing to leave. It had stared at them for a full minute before disappearing into the trees.

Before Abby could speak, Julea turned around and gasped. Her eyes popped open at the sight of the apples.

"What's wrong, Mom?" Abby asked.

"Oh! Nothing, Angel," Julea stammered momentarily. Her eyes suddenly glistened and she spoke quickly in a clear effort to stop herself from crying. "You must have found the Great Tree…I just love the apples grown here… on the Sider Farm. I should have known that my own daughter would too. Have you eaten any yet?" She wiped her eyes and smiled at Abby inquiringly.

Abby realized her mom was probably having some memory of Aunt Lacey that the apples brought up for her. *Oops.*

"Uh, yes. It's the most delicious apple I've ever eaten. I guess that's why they're called 'golden delicious' although I never tasted one from the grocers like this. It makes me wonder if the fruit we used to eat was really organic." Abby tried to distract her mom from thinking about Lacey by talking about food.

Her mother was a nutritionist. Being the child of a nutritionist made you very aware of what you consumed on a daily basis. Abby was sure she knew more about food than any other kid her age in the entire world.

She also knew a lot about sex for someone who had never done it. If Abby wasn't mistaken, Julea was bringing up just that subject now.

"Abby, you're at an age now that your body is going through changes," she was saying. "Please know you can come and talk to me anytime."

"Mom, I've had my period for two years now," said Abby. "And you've already told me all I need to know about sex and condoms. Don't worry, Mom. Besides, I don't even know any boys here." Abby pushed the picture of Cash diving into the river out of her mind.

"I know, Angel," replied Julea. "I mean other changes. Just know you can trust me to talk about anything. And I love you." Julea peered intently into Abby's eyes. She seemed to almost quiver before she finished. "And I'm so excited for you."

"What are you so excited about," laughed Abby. She decided her mom was seriously losing it.

"I don't know," sang Julea as she returned to her meal preparations. "I'm just excited."

Abby didn't know how her mom could go from looking like she was going to cry, to talking about sex, to grinning like a lunatic. *This must be how Mom deals with grief.* Abby headed upstairs to her room to get away from the weirdness.

Jack

Abby was true to her word. She didn't rat him out for tricking her. Jack was spared an uncomfortable lecture from his mother about what is and isn't appropriate to joke about. The death of his aunt would hang there silently in the background. But he would hear it loud and clear.

Next time he'd have to make sure the recipient of that particular prank knew how to swim, he decided. Perhaps the opportunity would arise soon, he thought, as he was introduced to his cousin that evening.

Travis was the same age as Jack. Their birthdays were only days apart. But other than that, Jack didn't think they had much in common. They looked drastically different. Travis wore his hair long. Jack was clean-cut. Travis wore sweatpants and a white t-shirt. Jack wore jeans and a black t-shirt.

Travis had barely said a word since he'd arrived with his father, Frank McAllister.

The senior McAllister was another mystery. The only thing Jack knew about him, was that he was a woodcarver. *Who was this man who fell in love with Aunt Lacey, and now raised their son by himself? Did he hate her now? Why didn't he come to the funeral?*

Jack figured he'd find out the details sooner or later. In the meantime, he still hadn't been in the barn yet. "Have you been in the barn, Cousin?" He asked.

Travis took a moment to register the question.

"Yes," said Travis. "Why?"

"I haven't but I've been meaning to," replied Jack. "Do you think you could show me around?" It was better than sitting around listening to their dads talk shop.

Travis agreed and the two boys headed out back. Their eyes adjusted to the moonlight as they approached the barn. Travis reached up expertly into the shadows inside the door.

A second later, there was light from a single bulb filling the space quite inadequately.

Jack followed Travis into the barn. He saw that it was large and spacious with high ceilings. There were ladders and a loft. There was also a whole lot of hay. It was full of hay, but it was designed for people, Jack saw. There were tables along one wall. Hay was piled in the corners for sitting on, Jack assumed.

"What happens in here?" he asked Travis.

"Oh, all sorts of things. Meetings, parties, the family reunion; or so I'm told."

Jack didn't need to ask why Travis hadn't attended a family reunion despite living nearby. No one under fourteen was allowed to attend. Abby was only ten months older than Jack. She'd missed the last reunion because of her September birthday. Next year would be their "Sacred Summer," as Mom called it. They would both attend the reunion for the first time together.

Jack realized it would be Travis's first family reunion too. "You coming?" He asked. He knew he didn't have to explain his question. The annual Sider reunions held a certain amount of awe for all family members under fourteen. They watched as their older cousins came back from their first gatherings changed. It was a rite of passage, steeped in mystery.

"Freakin' hippies," Jack mumbled under his breath. It was what his father called them.

"Yeah, I'm coming," replied Travis. "Dad said I'd get a gift at my first reunion. I'm so curious. But that's all he tells me. A very special gift that I don't want to miss out on, he says."

Jack's spirit rose. "I hope I get a gift too," he said. "I've been wanting a quad to ride. As soon as I knew we were going to live on a big piece of property, I told my parents they'd better get me a quad. I've been asking for one since I was old enough to say the word."

Travis smiled. "I've got my own and a spare. Want to go for a ride tomorrow?"

Malvis

It may be a mysterious family but it kept her in business doing what she loved, so she didn't ask any questions and what she did learn, she kept to herself. No sense in jeopardizing the mutually beneficial relationship between herself and the Siders just for some entertaining gossip.

Malvis O'Leary was a costume designer. She loved her work with a passion. As soon as Lacey Lynn learned there was a custom costume designer living in Beaverdell, she had come knocking.

That July, countless members of the Sider family came to her door, many ordering in advance. If she had not been blessed with daughters, there would have been no way to manage the workload.

Lacey Lynn had decided to hold a costume ball during the annual Sider family reunion that year. She invited the entire town. Only a few townspeople attended that first year but all those who didn't regretted it.

It was the largest, most outrageous party the town had ever seen. The following year, Malvis was overwhelmed with costume orders and had to turn many away. It horrified her to turn away business but she couldn't have accommodated them all in time.

Since then, Halloween had gotten more popular. Townspeople would purchase costumes for the Sider Costume Ball and use them again for Halloween. It helped them to rationalize the expense, Malvis guessed, if they could wear it more than once. Some preferred to purchase new for each occasion. She loved those customers.

Malvis was one of the few who attended the first ball. She cherished the opportunity to display her creations on her own family members. The costume ball was not just a party; it was a chance to advertise.

Yes, Malvis had a lot to be thankful for. When she'd moved with her husband to the small town of Beaverdell, she thought her costume design business would die. If it were not for Lacey Lynn, she might have had to give up a career that she loved.

Instead, her business tripled from what it was in the city. In exchange for a costume, Lacey's uncle built Malvis a website to promote her business and through which people could order her costumes from around the world.

She was currently working on a costume for Lacey's father. It was a wondrously beautiful eagle costume, using real eagle feathers that he supplied himself. How he ever collected all those feathers, Malvis could only imagine. But she never asked. She accepted the bounty eagerly as ideas for the costume danced merrily in her mind.

It was ten years since the first Sider Costume Ball, and orders on the website were continuous. Malvis was able to keep up by hiring her daughters. It pleased her to be able to pass down her knowledge. It pleased her daughters to make some extra money and have the attention of the townsfolk twice a year.

The Siders and all their various branches of the family tree comprised her most faithful customers, ordering all sorts of custom designs for every occasion. She'd made many of their wedding gowns, including Lacey's sister, Julea, who recently moved onto the Sider property.

Julea's wedding order was made online, so Malvis did not recognize the woman who now stood on her doorstep with her teenage daughter. But one look into the woman's eyes, and recognition dawned. Lacey's eyes. She'd recognize them anywhere.

"Hello, we've only met by email, but I'm Julea Sider," she said as she reached for Malvis' hand. "I wanted to thank you in person for my beautiful wedding gown and see if you could fit in an order for my daughter, Abby. It's short notice but we need it for September 10th."

Malvis smiled warmly at Julea and Abby. "Why, of course," she said as she ushered them in. "It would be my pleasure, I'm sure. And is there a special occasion then?"

"Not really," replied Abby. "Only in our family is the fourteenth birthday considered special."

Julea smiled. "Stop it, Abby," she said. "You know you're as excited as I am. Now pull out your notebook and show Malvis your designs."

SEPTEMBER 2008

Julea

As Abby's fourteenth birthday approached, Julea began preparations. She knew the dinner would be highly attended and wanted Abby to remember it fondly. She'd invited the McAllisters, of course. Duke and Darla were coming. Then there were the guests that only she would be aware of; the spirited, ancient, family members who secretly inhabited the property.

Julea had told the children and Michael about them, but they thought she was teasing. She couldn't help but laugh when they didn't believe her. *Oh well, they will know soon enough.*

Every time Julea thought about her family members, she thought of Lacey. Where could she be? Why hadn't anyone heard from her in so long?

I must stop obsessing about this. I must focus. First Abby's birthday and everything that will come after. And soon enough, the day when Michael's eyes will finally be opened.

***

The first day of school, Julea walked her children to the bus stop. It was a bit of a hike to the bridge that joined the

Sider Farm to the McAllister property and the main road that ran through it.

Normally, she would have driven them to their first day at a new school. But she couldn't bring herself to leave the land for the hour drive down gravel road to town. Being home was like being given an endless supply of water and realizing you've been dying of thirst. Pure relaxation and calm came over her. She knew the kids first day of school would be fine.

Four McAllister children unexpectedly met them at the small, wooden bridge built in some distant past by one of their esteemed ancestors. Julea guessed that Travis passed the word since he and Jack had developed a quick and easy friendship over the past month.

As they walked, Julea admitted to herself that it was hard to see Lacey's son and be reminded of her sister. She could not accept that Lacey might be dead. Lacey was a survivor. A warrior. Her power was too strong to be overcome. But where was she then?

Julea's thoughts were distracted by her daughter's scream. A wolf stood in their path, tongue lolling and eyes bright. It was looking at Abby. The other children froze for a moment before Travis took the situation in hand.

"Oh, get out of here," he said to the wolf and waved his arm contemptuously. The wolf seemed to smile, then turned and trotted off into the trees. Abby walked over to Julea and joined arms.

"Mama, that was too freaky," she said under her breath.

"Don't worry about him," said Cathryn. "He won't hurt you. He'll just annoy the rest of us, is all."

Julea squeezed her daughter's arm. "He seemed pretty friendly to me," she assured Abby.

Julea smiled to herself. *This was just the beginning.*

Abby

Abby wondered where Cash was when the rest of the McAllister children met them at the bridge. She kept the disappointment off her face in case her mom caught on. When she saw the wolf and screamed, she was glad Cash wasn't there to witness her girly reaction. No one else had freaked out.

He came running up to the bus just as it arrived. Abby was sure her mom couldn't have missed the way Cash smiled at her and said "Good morning, Abby." Or how Abby's face had burned red as she replied a timid "good morning" back and giggled.

She had to give Mom credit though because she didn't betray herself at all. She simply turned to the eldest McAllister sibling and asked him to "take care of my children today, please." Abby silently worshipped her mother for a moment before kissing her goodbye and boarding the bus.

Jack walked with Travis to the back of the empty bus. Abby followed her brother and chose a seat by herself. Cash slid in beside her. For the second time in a week, Abby felt electricity zap through her veins. She took a deep breath and steeled herself to be calm.

Cathryn, Kenny, and Olivia crowded around them. They began telling Abby about the school. Abby tried to listen but she was distracted by the wild and mischievous

Cash McAllister. His wavy, overgrown hair hung unself-consciously to his shoulders. He sat up straight but his shoulders appeared relaxed and confident. Abby wondered if he had a girlfriend.

When they got closer to town, the bus stopped at each street to pick up some children along the way. Cash introduced Abby and Jack to each new face as they peered curiously over the backs of their chairs at the new students.

Abby was feeling optimistic about her first day at the new school, when a sneering voice came from the crowd. "Is that your new girlfriend, Cash? What happened to you and Mona?"

Abby's cheeks burned. She knew he must have a girlfriend. What guy who looked like him wouldn't have a dozen girls after him?

"Shut your pie-hole, Jeremy," rebutted Cathryn. "You're just jealous because no girl wants to sit next to you." Abby laughed nervously earning a dirty look from Jeremy.

"I'm not jealous," he spat. "She's nothing special." Now Abby felt sick. This was becoming embarrassing and mean. She hung her head hoping her bangs would hide her face a little. She did not like this kind of attention at all.

"Hey, watch what you say about my sister," Jack jumped up in her defense. Good old Jack, she thought, making an even bigger scene. And fighting on the first day of school. Michael was not going to like this.

Jeremy faced off with Jack. "What are you going to do about it?" he said quietly enough so that the bus driver couldn't hear him.

"You're going to find out…" Jack started to say when Cash interrupted him.

"Jeremy, man. Back off on the new kids," he said. "I've heard about Jack and you don't want to mess with him. He'll kick your sorry ass."

"My sister will kick your sorry ass," Jack chimed in. Abby groaned inwardly. She'd never been in a fight in her life.

Jeremy's sneer widened. "Ooh, I'm so scared," he mocked. "Whatever, Cash. I'll leave your girlfriend alone. I just hope you don't break Mona's heart. On second thought, I hope you do. Then we can see how tough your new girlfriend is. Gotta love a catfight."

Jeremy turned back to his friends. Abby continued to hang her head hoping no one was looking at her.

"Just ignore him," Cash whispered. He reached over and squeezed her hand. "He can't help it. He probably descends from a long line of jackasses."

Abby lifted her chin and looked Cash in the eye. "He doesn't scare me," she said. *But you do,* she thought in her head. *Yes, you do.*

***

After school, Abby didn't go straight home. She said goodbye to the McAllisters at the bridge without looking at Cash. She assured Jack he could go on ahead of her, then walked down to the clearing by the river.

As she passed the massive, ancient apple tree, she heard another apple fall. She walked towards it this time, scooping it up and digging her teeth into it. Flavour again burst inside her mouth. She felt like her eyesight grew sharper. The colours around her appeared brighter. These were some amazing apples, she chuckled to herself.

At the river, Abby sat down beside a tree and watched the current until she'd finished her apple. She lied back in the grass and closed her eyes. It had been a good day. A long day, but a good day. The teachers seemed nice. She'd made a few new friends out of the girls near her age. Cathryn stuck by her side all day. She liked Cathryn.

She also liked Cash. *A lot.*

Mona was waiting for Cash when they arrived at the school. Abby fervently hoped that Mona would turn out to be a cat or at worst, an ex-girlfriend. But it was as she'd feared. Mona was a real person and she was Cash's girlfriend.

Why am I getting so caught up over a boy I just met? Abby scolded herself. *This is ridiculous.* But when she remembered Mona walking up to Cash and wrapping her arms around his neck for a kiss, she felt tears sting her eyes. She'd avoided Cash for the rest of the day and made sure to sit with Cathryn on the bus ride home.

Oh well, sighed Abby. Nothing I can do about it. She opened her eyes, stretched and sat up. There, staring at her from across the river, was the wolf she'd seen in the morning.

Abby felt much safer with the river between them. She smiled this time. "Why, hello there," she greeted the canine.

He cocked his head at her and smiled. At least that was what it looked like he was doing. Although whether it was a smile or not, Abby really couldn't say.

"You sure are friendly," she said. The wolf lied down and rolled over making Abby laugh. "You're cute too. And you know it." Abby wondered if her parents would believe her when she told them about this.

Suddenly the wolf's ears perked. He stood up and turned to walk away. When he got to the trees, he stopped and looked back.

"See ya later," Abby waved. The wolf turned and loped off into the trees.

***

The next few days before Abby's birthday continued the same. The McAllister children met them at the bridge and walked them to the bus. Cash arrived at the last minute and said good morning to Abby. Abby said good morning back then spent the rest of the day avoiding Cash as much as possible.

At the end of each day, Abby stopped at the river on her way home. Inevitably, the wolf that lived on the McAllister property would sit across the water from her and they would have a one-sided conversation.

Abby enjoyed the time with "her wolf," as she'd come to think of him. Although Abby knew it was impossible for him to understand what she was saying, she couldn't help feeling like he recognized every word. He stared at her with knowing eyes and even seemed to respond in human ways to some of the things she said, nodding his head at times or emitting a wolfish sound that suited whatever she was talking about.

At first, she wasn't sure if this was the same wolf she'd seen on her first day of school. It was Cathryn McAllister who confirmed it for her when the wolf once again interrupted their walk to the bus. The girls had fallen behind the rest of the group when Abby's wolf stepped out in front of them.

"Don't you have better things to do?" Cathryn huffed at the wolf. "We don't need a chaperone, you know." She turned to Abby and rolled her eyes. "I think he likes you."

"Is he your pet?" Abby asked.

Cathryn seemed uncomfortable. "Not really. We have lots of wolves on our land," she said evasively. "But they usually stay out of sight when people are around."

Accustomed to the wolf, and boldened by Cathryn's obvious lack of fear, Abby held out her hand. The wolf approached and let her pet his head. Abby thrilled at the feel of his fur and giggled when he flicked his head up to lick her face. Cathryn groaned.

The wolf padded along beside them for a few minutes before disappearing into the woods.

"So, are you excited about your birthday?" Cathryn asked after he was gone.

"I guess so," replied Abby. "I mean, it seems a little weird to make such a big deal out of my fourteenth birthday but I'm glad you're coming over." She smiled at her new friend.

"Fourteen is a big one in our family too," Cathryn confided. "Not so much the day but the age. We don't throw a big celebration or anything but we get a big gift close to our fourteenth birthday. I'm sick of watching Cash flaunt his gift in front of my face."

"What did he get?" asked Abby.

Cathryn was silent for a moment. Then she whispered. *"Freedom."* She looked at Abby penetratingly. "We get freedom when we're fourteen."

Abby wanted to ask more, but they'd arrived at the bus stop and Cash was running towards them. "Good morning, Abby," he grinned widely at her.

"Good morning," she mumbled uncomfortably. She boarded the bus with Cathryn and their conversation turned to school and boys. All boys except Cash, that is. Abby couldn't bear to speak of the one boy who filled her thoughts night and day.

Cash

As he walked with his family to the Sider house for her birthday dinner, Cash pondered his strange interest in Abby. Ever since he'd met her on the bridge that day, he'd been unable to stop thinking about her.

He knew he would have to break things off with Mona soon. He wanted Abby to be his girlfriend and he would need some time between them if he was going to spare Mona's feelings.

He wasn't even sure if Abby was interested in him. She seemed to go out of her way to avoid him on the bus and at school. But he was determined to win her over. Tonight, he would start by giving her a birthday present. It was a small wooden wolf, hand-crafted by his Uncle Frank.

Cash had carved a small heart on the bottom, so his intentions would not be misunderstood. It was the heart that made him so nervous. He wasn't even sure he'd have the guts to give her the gift after all.

It wasn't just that she was pretty and had an amazing smile. Cash felt an overwhelming urge to protect and take care of her. It couldn't have anything to do with the treaty since he didn't feel that way about the other Sider-Bagwells. Cash wondered if Abby even knew about the treaty.

At night, he dreamed of her. Wild, fitful dreams that always ended with him shielding her from bullets or dragging her from a fire or some other danger. Sometimes his dreams of her were sweeter, filled with kisses. He awoke every morning thinking of her.

They arrived at the house and Angus knocked on the door. Jack opened it, inviting them in. Julea strode into the entrance-way to welcome them.

"I'm so glad you could make it," she gushed. "My baby's all grown up now and we are happy to share the event with our closest friends. Thank you so much for bringing salad, Janine," she said as she took the bowl from Cash's mother.

"You're welcome," beamed Janine. "You all are family and we wouldn't miss it for the world." While Julea ushered the McAllisters into the living room, Cash watched his younger brother Kenny disappear up the stairs with Jack and Travis.

"And where is the birthday girl?" Angus' voice boomed.

"She's still getting ready," smiled Julea. "You know girls. Cathryn and Olivia, you are welcome to go find her if you'd like. She's up in her room." Cash watched his sisters disappear up the stairs too.

Cash sat down with the adults and waited anxiously for Abby to join them. He paid little attention to the conversation, focusing instead on keeping his eyes away from the stairway. He looked around the room examining one plant at a time. The Siders clearly loved their plants. *There must be fifty in this room alone.* Cash hid his small, wrapped gift behind a porcelain shoe full of begonias on the table beside him.

"I see you've noticed our plants." Julea's voice startled Cash from his task.

"Ah, yes, they are very beautiful," Cash responded politely. "And so lush. You must take really good care of them."

Julea seemed pleased with his observations. "Well, I can't take all the credit but I do agree that they're beautiful," she said. "How old are you now, Cash?"

"He's almost fifteen," Angus replied for him. "He's not a pup anymore." He winked at Julea and Janine nodded her head. Julea gazed at Cash with interest. Cash was beginning to feel self-conscious when Michael interrupted.

"Speaking of dogs," said Michael. "Abby says you've got wolves on your land, Angus."

Angus shot a brief quizzical look at Julea. Almost imperceptibly, she shook her head.

"Why yes we do," he said turning to Michael. "They're quite tame though, if you're concerned about it. We've been sharing the land for a long time and we've come to an understanding."

"That's good to know," replied Michael. "One of those wolves is following Abby around and I wasn't sure if it was safe, although Julea seems to think it's fine."

"Yeah, I heard about that from Cathryn," said Angus, glancing at Cash. "I can assure you that Abby is quite safe with that particular wolf. Cash also has a relationship with that one. What do you say, Cash?"

Cash nodded in agreement. "Oh yes, sir," he said. "She's totally safe with him." Cash was distracted while he was speaking by a movement he saw out of the corner of his eye. He looked at the table beside him. The gift he'd brought for Abby was gone.

Michael did not seem convinced about the wolf but let it go for the moment, as Abby, Cathryn, and Olivia came skipping down the stairs. Cash's heart pounded. *Where was the gift?*

He caught his breath when he saw Abby. She wore a burgundy, strapless satin dress that was fitted on top and hung loose to her knees. Her hair was curled in ringlets around her face. She wore long, silver earrings shaped like feathers that sparkled in the lamplight.

"Well, here's the birthday girl," grinned Angus. "You look stunning, little darlin'. I think Cash will need to wipe the drool off his chin." Cash shot his dad a shocked look and noticed Abby's dad squinting in his direction. *Oh great,* he inwardly groaned.

Abby blushed and thanked Angus for the compliment. She quickly sat down beside her mother, keeping her eyes averted from Cash.

The conversation turned to less prickly subjects such as how the Sider-Bagwells were settling into the old homestead. Cash pretended interest in the plants beside him again, while he searched for the gift he'd lost. Perhaps it fell back behind the table. He leaned down to look.

"What are you looking for, Cash?" his sister asked quietly so she wouldn't interrupt the adults.

"Oh, nothing," he said quickly glancing at Abby. "I thought I dropped something." Cathryn gave him a puzzled look, then shrugged. Jack, Travis, and Kenny appeared again at the bottom of the stairs.

"We're going out to the barn," said Kenny, as the three of them headed towards the back door.

"Good idea," Julea said, as she jumped out of her seat. "Why don't you all go?" Cash didn't want to leave the living room without the gift, but he didn't want Abby to go without him either. He decided he'd look for it again when there were less people in the living room, maybe during dinner.

The barn was decorated for the occasion with balloons, streamers, strings of lights, and a large "Happy Birthday" banner that hung from the rafters across the barn. Even Abby seemed surprised when they entered the brightly lit barn.

"When did Mom and Michael do this?" she wondered aloud.

"I don't know," said Jack. "I have no idea."

Julea's voice came from the doorway behind them. "Do you like it, Angel?" she asked. "We always hold our celebrations in the barn. This is where we'll eat tonight." She turned to a table beside her and switched on the radio. "You guys can listen to whatever you want. We'll be out in a bit to join you."

Abby

The evening had been exhilarating. It was hard to believe a night could be so amazing. The barn was decorated extensively just for her. She'd laughed, danced, talked, and smiled so much her cheeks hurt. Cash paid attention to her all night.

There was a moment when she'd gone into the house to get a sweater and Cash was coming out of the living room that they passed each other, their bodies almost touching. They lingered and Abby thought Cash might kiss her as she gazed up into his eyes. Electricity shot through the air between them. But they each kept walking and the moment passed.

When she climbed into bed that night, Abby found one last gift tucked under her pillow. It was wrapped in shiny silver paper. The tag said *"To Abby, From Cash."* She unwrapped the paper and found a hand-carved wolf with a heart engraved into the bottom of it. She squeezed the wolf tightly, letting pure pleasure wash over her. This was a birthday Abby would never forget.

Cash

Monday morning on the bus, Cash was preoccupied. He didn't find the gift before leaving Abby's house and was nervous about that. She smiled shyly at the bus stop, but hadn't looked at him again.

He was also nervous about breaking up with Mona. It had to be done. He'd almost kissed Abby on Saturday night. He had to end things with Mona before anything like that happened again. It wasn't his way to two-time someone. That is, if Abby ever lets him near enough to almost kiss her again.

He glanced back at her where she sat with Cathryn and some of the other girls their age. It was what he did lately. He watched Abby. He would have felt like a fool if he wasn't enjoying it so much.

***

On second break, many of the students congregated on the bridge deck near the school as was customary. Cash noticed that Mona didn't come out and felt a twinge of regret for hurting her. Abby was there, though. Seeing her smile warmed his heart. He was too nervous to approach her and didn't want to embarrass Mona by doing so. But he was very aware of Abby's every move that day.

So, when Jeremy Jones began to hassle Abby, Cash picked up on it right away. Jeremy was teasing Abby's friends, pretending he was going to push them off the bridge. The girls giggled and dodged him, but Abby didn't find it funny.

"Don't you dare push me," Abby commanded in a raised voice. Cash could see that her words only made Jeremy more determined.

"Hey Jeremy," he yelled. "Why don't you pick on someone your own size?" Jeremy looked at Cash and backed off. He walked away from Abby to join his friends again. Cash turned back to his own friends so he wouldn't appear too concerned about Abby in front of the others.

But a moment later, he heard a splash. When he turned around, Jeremy stood in Abby's place looking down into the river. Abby was *gone.*

In two large strides Cash went diving over the side of the bridge. He remembered the first day he'd met Abby when she admitted she couldn't swim. The water hit him like a punch in the face. Abby was nowhere to be seen. He came up to the surface looking frantically for her and diving under again, but the only trace of her was a floating sneaker.

On his third try, he came up for air to find the sky turning black before his eyes. A deafening noise enveloped him. Hundreds ... no, thousands ... of crows flew and squawked overhead. For several moments, he treaded water while he stared transfixed. Waves upon waves of crows blackened out the sky.

As the last of the birds flew over the children's heads, Cash remembered where he was. He scanned the water for Abby again. This time he saw her.

She was about a mile downriver. Her head was turned to him and for a brief moment their eyes met. Then she disappeared.

Abby

Abby heard about it on first break. The story went that Cash had taken Mona aside in the morning and told her he wanted to break up. Mona was in the girl's washroom crying and hadn't come out. Although Abby felt sorry for

Mona, she could hardly stop smiling. She thought nothing could bring down her high spirits until on second break, when Jeremy Jones introduced her to her destiny.

Abby didn't have time to react. She'd been staring down at the water silently thanking Cash for telling Jeremy to leave her alone. She would be so humiliated if he'd pushed her into the water. Everyone would see that she couldn't swim. She'd probably thrash like a freak right before she drowned. Lost in thought, she suddenly felt hands on her back, heard her girlfriends scream belatedly, and then, she was falling.

As the river came closer, Abby realized that Jeremy had decided to push her after all. This was how her life would end. She was very calm as she descended. She accepted her fate. She thought about how dying wasn't as scary as she'd thought it would be. Then she hit the water.

The moment her body was submerged she felt the transition begin. Waves of exhilaration pulsed through her body. It felt like the most natural thing in the world. Like the water was a part of her.

She looked up towards the people on the bridge and realized she was still under water. She was breathing under water. *Or she was dead.* Abby looked down at her body. Where her legs should have been, she saw a fish tail fluttering softly. She became confused. But Abby didn't have time to figure it out. Her instincts screamed at her to get away before anyone else could see what had become of her.

As she darted away, she noticed Cash swimming above her, calling her name. Her heart burst with love for him. A moment later, she couldn't help but look back at him. She resurfaced to the shock of crows filling the air above her. Looking towards the bridge, she was startled at how far she'd come in mere seconds.

There was Cash. One head bobbing in the water with a backdrop of children, lined up on the bridge, looking into the sky. As Abby decided to leave, Cash looked her way. Their eyes met and something profound ignited in Abby's heart. Fearing the others would see her too; she dove gracefully into the river depths and made her way quickly home.

***

As Abby climbed out of the river, her scales became legs. The process was so amazing that she had to keep putting her legs back in the water to see it happen all over again. Her clothes disappeared and reappeared soaking wet each time she went through the change.

When she finally stood up to walk home, she couldn't stop herself from turning back around and diving into the river again. *Just to make sure,* she told herself.

Abby didn't think her mom would believe her, but she would bring her back and show her if needed. She'd lost one shoe in the fall, so she walked awkwardly up the path towards her house, relieved that Michael was nowhere in sight.

So caught up in her thoughts, she was almost at the house before she noticed the crows. She turned around, her eyes widening at the sight. They were everywhere. They filled the branches of every tree on the property.

Every little beady eye stared at her as she ambled up the path. Silently, they watched her walk all the way to the door.

Abby could hear her mother and several other women's voices in the kitchen. She snuck upstairs to put some dry clothes on. Quietly, she approached the kitchen door, straining to hear who was there with her mother. The voices were vaguely familiar but Abby was flustered from her experience and couldn't place them. She was startled to hear her mother crying.

"What else can it mean?" Julea sniffed. "The 'winged darkness' has befallen."

"But we cannot have failed," said a woman's voice that didn't belong to Abby's mother. "We have worked so hard. I was sure that change is happening."

"It is happening but not fast enough," said another strangely familiar female voice. "Word is coming back from the allied forts. They all report the same. 'Winged darkness' has indeed befallen."

"If this is it, then the Final Chosen One received her powers," said yet another voice. "I wonder who it is?"

There was complete silence in the room for a moment. Abby decided it was time to go in. As she opened the door, she was surprised to find her mother sitting alone.

Julea

Julea stared in astonishment as her daughter walked into the room.

"Mom, where'd they go?" she said anxiously. "I heard voices in here only a moment ago. Who was it?"

Julea wiped away tears and looked into Abby's eyes. "Abby, Honey, what are you doing home from school? Did something happen?"

Just then, the phone rang. Julea looked at the call display and saw it was the school. She answered.

"Hi Julea, it's Jackie Logan here. Abby didn't return to school after lunch and I wanted to make sure she's safe."

"Yes, she's here," Julea assured Principal Logan. "She wasn't feeling well. I was just about to call you."

"There's something else," said Mrs. Logan. "It's about Jack. He was fighting this afternoon. The other boy looks pretty bad. Neither of them will tell us why the fight occurred. In fact, none of the kids are talking. I'm sorry but we're going to have to suspend Jack. Can you please come and pick him up?"

"Of course," said Julea. As she hung up the phone, she turned to look at Abby. "What happened today?" she asked again.

Abby

Abby didn't know what she expected when she told her mom that she was a mermaid, but it wasn't this. Her mother's eyes popped open in surprise. She grinned big and said, "Well, we didn't see that coming, did we?"

"I'm not lying, Mom." Maybe her mom didn't understand.

"Of course, you aren't," Julea laughed. She jumped up and put her arms around Abby. "If I'd known you'd be a mermaid, I wouldn't have wasted all that time fighting with you about swimming lessons," she cried.

"Mom. What are you talking about?" Abby was disconcerted that her mother was taking the news so well. "Why aren't you freaking out?"

Julea pulled back from Abby and took her face in her hands. She looked her daughter in the eyes. "Honey, I have so much to tell you but we have to go pick up your brother. Let's go and I'll tell you what I can during the drive to the school."

PART TWO

INSTINCTS

Should you fail in your tasks, winged darkness shall befall you.
On the day that darkness doth descend, the Final Chosen One
will receive her powers. It shall be a sign unto all
that The End Days are upon you.

Abby

Abby sat beside her mother in the front passenger seat of their car. It was an hour drive to the high school down a bumpy dirt road. As they pulled away from the house, her mother began to speak.

"When descendants of the Sider family turn fourteen, we are brought to the Sider Farm to receive our powers. Usually during our first family reunion. That's why we call it the "Sacred Summer," she explained. "We eat one of the apples from the Great Tree by the river. Then we all wait to see what happens."

"I've been eating those apples almost every day since we arrived," said Abby.

"I know and since you turned fourteen, I knew it could be any day for you," agreed Julea.

"But why didn't you tell me, Mama?"

"Well, for one thing, it can interfere with the change if a person is aware of it ahead of time. But more importantly, we don't want to burden you with The Knowledge of The Cause until you've received your powers."

Abby was confused. "What knowledge? What cause?" she sputtered.

"I'm sorry, Angel," said Julea. "This is my first time sharing the story with one of my children and I'm probably not doing it right. Usually, the whole thing is explained at the Fire of the Elders. The Cause is our destiny. Our fate. Our family is part of something very big. Something very important."

At those words, Abby felt her heart rate rise. "What, Mama?" she asked.

"All I will tell you now is that you will be compelled by an infinite power to live and die for The Cause as soon as you've learned what it is. I want you to have a few months to enjoy your powers before you receive The Knowledge."

Abby was beginning to feel like someone was playing a joke on her. This all seemed unreal. Then a thought occurred to her.

"Will Jack get powers too?" she asked.

"Yes, he will. But don't tell him about yours in the meantime. You must hide your powers until the family reunion, and even then, we all lay low until the new recruits receive theirs. Next year will be Jack's Sacred Summer. It is an important rite of passage."

"We?" Abby stammered. "You mean you have powers too, Mama?"

"Yes," her mother replied. "It is because of our powers that we are a matriarchy."

"You mean how the Sider women keep their last name and pass it onto their children?"

"Yes," her mother replied. "When a woman has carried a child in her womb, there can be no question as to who the mother is. But there is always a chance that the father isn't really the father…"

Abby interrupted her mother because she didn't need another lecture about sex. "Why does Jack have Michael's last name then?"

Her mother was silent for a moment. "That was a personal decision that Michael and I made together. He wanted his son to pass on the family name like most people do in the straight world…um, I mean traditional western culture."

Abby could just imagine how that argument went. Michael was very stern about conforming to society's expectations. Whereas Mom would just be glad if they ate, Michael would require sitting properly, eating with utensils, and asking for permission to leave the table. Whereas Mom would just giggle at bathroom humour, Michael would demand that such topics not be discussed. No wonder Mom gave in to giving Jack the Bagwell name. Michael would never have forgiven her if she hadn't.

Abby changed the subject. "So, you're a mermaid too?"

"No, Honey, we all receive different powers depending on what our destined role will be in The Cause. My other form is a unicorn and my task is related to healing."

"What is my task if I am a mermaid, Mom?"

"Let's not talk about that yet, Angel," Julea replied. "You will learn everything at the family reunion next July. For now, you must focus on learning how to use your powers. And enjoying them."

Jack

News travelled fast in the small high school. Jack was at the store when it happened. Before he'd finished paying for his bottled water and potato chips, Travis was at his side telling him the story. Jeremy Jones pushed Abby off the bridge.

Jack's first instinct was fear. Was Abby okay? Where was she now? Travis didn't have any answers. At least his answers weren't good enough for Jack. He didn't know where Abby was or if she was okay. He told Jack that Cash had jumped in knowing she didn't swim well, but he'd climbed out of the water without her.

That was all Travis knew.

Jack's next feeling was pure rage. He stalked out of the store; his eyes peeled for Jeremy Jones. As he approached the bridge, he noticed the crowd was much bigger than usual. One look at Jack, and everyone moved out of his way. They opened a path right up to Jeremy Jones.

Jeremy looked scared but determined not to back down. Jack didn't even give him a chance to explain. He took two steps for momentum and landed a flying side-kick in the centre of Jeremy's chest. With an "oof," Jeremy fell onto his back several feet away.

Jack continued to walk towards him. Red-faced, Jeremy scrambled to his feet, and attempted to speak. "I didn't know she can't..." His voice broke off as Jack's left fist bounced off his cheek, sending spit flying out of the side of Jeremy's mouth.

"I told you to leave my sister alone," Jack said between clenched teeth. Before Jeremy could respond, Jack punched him with his right. Jeremy hit the pavement again, blood spilling from his nose.

"Stop, man, please. I'm sorry," Jeremy begged as he pulled himself to his feet again. Jack was too angry for apologies. One last solid kick square in the chest sent Jeremy over the side of the bridge into the water.

As Jeremy's friends rushed down the bank to help him, Jack turned to the crowd. Horrified faces stared back at him. He looked back at them refusing to be intimidated or show weakness. His eyes settled on Cash who stood dripping off to the side near the embankment.

"Where's my sister?" he asked the eldest McAllister child.

"I don't know," replied Cash. "I thought I saw her way downriver but then she disappeared." Jack's heart skipped a beat. *Disappeared?*

"She can't swim," he told Cash.

"I know, man," said Cash. "That's why I jumped in."

Jack's eyes filled with tears. "Thank you," he said. There was an uncomfortable silence. Jack got the feeling that someone was standing behind him. He turned around. It was Principal Logan.

"What's going on here?" she said to the crowd. No one answered. She gestured to Jeremy who had dragged himself up onto the bridge deck with the help of his friends. "I see a boy who is bleeding and soaking wet, and no one can tell me what happened?" Once again, her question was met with silence.

"Jeremy, who did this to you?" she asked. Jeremy did not answer. A girl who stood beside him did.

"It was Jack," she said.

Principal Logan turned to Jack. "Is this true, Jack?"

Jack tried very hard to hold it in, but he couldn't anymore. Tears streamed out of his eyes, as he looked Mrs. Logan full in the face. "Yes," he admitted.

"Both of you, please come with me," she said. She turned around and walked toward the school. Jack and Jeremy followed.

Over the next half hour, Jack and Jeremy both resisted Principal Logan's attempts to get the story out of them. Jack knew that if anything happened to Abby, the truth would come out eventually. In the meantime, he wasn't going to be the rat. He begrudgingly admitted to himself that Jeremy was no rat either.

When a teacher reported to Mrs. Logan that Abby hadn't returned to class after break, Jack's worry grew. He sat quietly listening while his mother was called. Tears fell unbidden again, when he heard with relief that Abby was with his mother. Jeremy also looked relieved, and some of the rage that had overtaken Jack earlier came back. He glared at the boy who had pushed his sister into the water. Jeremy wouldn't look at him. Principal Logan, however, saw the glare.

"Did this fight have something to do with Abby?" she asked. When neither boy answered her, she shrugged. "Well, if you aren't going to cooperate, you leave me with no other choice. You're both suspended for a week. Jack, your mother is on her way to pick you up. You can wait in the hall for her. Jeremy, stay put and I will call your parents right now."

Jack walked out of the office, crumpled onto a bench in the hallway and used all his strength to stop himself from crying. Abby is safe, he told himself repeatedly to calm his racing heart. It's okay, she's okay. But it was no use. He gave in to the tears for a few minutes; shuddering silently, with his head down, in plain view of anyone who passed. By the time his mother and sister arrived, he was in control of himself. He left the building with his head held high.

On the drive home, Jack explained why he'd been fighting. He knew his mother wouldn't punish him for defending his sister.

"But how'd you get home?" he asked Abby.

Before she could speak, his mother answered. "Abby's not such a bad swimmer after all," she said.

The rest of the drive was spent mostly in silence. Jack had what some people call "fighter's remorse." He was feeling bad about hurting Jeremy. Now that he knew his sister was okay and everything had worked out fine, he began to regret beating up the bully.

As they got closer to home, Jack's mother spoke.

"Something's happened, Jack," she said. Her voice sounded strange, sad and matter-of-fact at the same time. "As you'll see when we get home, we have some unwelcome visitors."

"What do you mean?" Jack asked. "Are Nana and Grandad here?" He knew his mother wasn't overly-fond of his father's parents.

Julea laughed nervously. "No, it's not your grandparents," she said.

"You mean the crows, Mom?" asked Abby.

"Yes, I mean the crows," she replied. "A huge flock of crows has landed on our property."

"You mean 'murder,'" replied Jack. "It's called 'a murder of crows.'" His mother didn't answer but she seemed to flinch.

"They flew over us right after I fell in the water," Abby added. "I wonder why they settled on our land?"

Their mother remained silent. Jack was confused. What was the big deal about a bunch of crows? But as they pulled up to the house, he saw what was the big deal. This wasn't just a few crows. There were hundreds of them sitting on every branch, in every tree on the property. They stared down at the Sider-Bagwell family with their beady eyes as they drove up the driveway and climbed out of the car. It made Jack's skin crawl.

Dad was in the yard, soaking wet, running around screaming and waving his arms like a lunatic among the trees. The crows didn't move. They ignored Michael, focusing instead on Abby, Jack and Julea as they walked toward the house.

"Julea," said Michael impatiently. "They won't budge. Where is the bull horn?" Jack looked at his mother and for the first time noticed that her eyes were wet.

"It's in the kitchen, in the cupboard over the sink," she replied. "But I doubt it will scare them," she said.

"What do you mean, it won't scare them?" Michael scoffed. "I'm not sure why they picked our place to rest but I'm not going to stand by and let them crap all over the apples." He strode purposefully towards the house.

Julea sighed and followed him. "It's okay, Mom," Jack rushed to comfort her. He put his arm around her shoulders. "Dad will get rid of them," he said. "And I'm sorry for getting in trouble."

Julea looked at her son. "I'm okay, Jack," she said lovingly. "I'm glad you stood up for your sister. And I hope you're right about the crows. I'm just feeling a little emotional today," she explained.

Jack didn't know what to say to that. He hugged his mom and kissed her on the cheek. "I love you, Mom," he said.

"I love you too, Baby," she replied. She turned and walked up the steps into the house. Jack decided to stay outside and watch his dad chase the crows away. As he scanned the trees around the house, he was astounded again by how many there were. They stared back at him with solemn, unafraid expressions. Jack began to doubt that the crows were going anywhere, bull horn or not.

Cash

Realizing he couldn't go back to class dripping wet and more than a little curious about what happened to Abby, Cash melted out of the crowd before Principal Logan could notice him. He walked into the trees beside the road and headed towards the Sider property.

He was following the road, hidden among the trees when he heard a car coming. As the car passed by, a rush of relief came over him. It was Julea's car and Abby was in the passenger seat. She'd made it home after all. Cash was impressed. How anyone could swim that far was beyond him. How a girl who couldn't swim had made it, he couldn't guess.

When he got near the Sider lands, Cash was startled to hear Michael's voice yelling loudly from the orchard. "Get out of here! Get out of here!"

Staying out of sight in the trees, Cash saw the crows before he saw Michael. Sitting among the branches, they chattered amongst themselves, preening, and getting comfortable. As Cash came padding through their ranks, they greeted him with a chorus of caws. They seemed to bow down as he passed. But that was ridiculous, and Cash dismissed the idea quickly.

He sniffed the air. He'd stopped yelling but Michael was close. Creeping more carefully, Cash peered through the trees. Michael was unravelling a hose. He turned the water on and walked toward one of the trees. As he raised the hose, the whole mass of crows that were perched in the tree flew into the air over Michael's head. All at once, they let their poop fly, literally. Michael was covered in crow feces from his head to his toes.

Michael's curses echoed off the mountains. Cash took advantage of the distraction and slipped past Michael to cross the bridge back to his own property. As he walked the last bit home, he couldn't shake a bad feeling that had come over him. He sensed that the crows were trying to tell him something. Like he was supposed to do something but he wasn't sure what.

Abby

From the moment her grandmother, great aunts, and mother's two cousins arrived, they'd holed up in the kitchen whispering conspiratorially.

Each of them had expressed her congratulations privately to Abby. Grandma Dianna gave her a big hug and lowered her voice, "I heard about your swimming experience, Abby. You'll have to show me some of your tricks while I'm here."

Mom's cousin, Aunty Jessica gave her a book called 'Water Warriors' by Matthew Collins. "Matthew's supernatural form is a merman," she said. "He wrote this book. It will tell you important things you need to know about your powers."

"You mean there's more to it than swimming?"

"Yes, Abby, there is much more to it than swimming," she said. "Make sure you read it carefully.

Abby couldn't wait to show off her skills to Grandma Dianna. She'd been down at the river the night before when everyone else was in bed. She undressed on the bank of the river, and dove in. As her body sliced into the water, she felt the exultant surge of freedom that came with the change.

Julea allowed Abby to take the week off with Jack while he was suspended so she could practice at night and sleep during the day. Abby enjoyed herself so much that first night, she barely made it home before sunrise.

Abby had never thought of her human form as restrictive before, but it was like a weight was lifted each time she phased into her scales. She could suddenly move easier, see better, and hear better. In fact, everything about her was stronger in her mermaid form.

On Tuesday, Abby woke late. She'd swum vigorously the night before. Her muscles ached but Abby savoured the pain. She could feel her muscles strengthening, even in her human form.

Groggily, she headed downstairs for a snack. Grandma Dianna must have heard her coming, because she opened the kitchen door, handed Abby a slice of pie, and told her to run along until dinner.

Abby noticed the sun was shining and headed out to sit on the porch while she ate. She was almost finished her pie when she heard a voice.

"Are you planning to come back to school ever again?"

Abby looked up to find Cash McAllister standing a few yards away, staring at her with a peculiar expression on his face. He was holding her shoe.

"Oh," she started from her seat, self-consciously reaching for her hair. She forced her hand to her side. "Ah, yes, I'm coming back next week." Cash set her sneaker on the porch steps.

"I'm glad to see that you're okay," he said. "I guess you're a better swimmer than you realized."

Abby didn't know what to say. Before she could answer, Cash spoke again.

"We've missed you at school," he said shyly. Then more firmly, "That is, I've missed you." He smiled crookedly at her.

Abby felt like she might melt on the spot. Her heart hammered in her chest. "Um, thank you for jumping in to save me."

"You're welcome. I mean, I didn't do anything. But I couldn't stand by and do nothing," Cash replied. "Are you busy right now? Want to take a walk down to the river?"

"Uh, sure," said Abby. "Just let me run in and change my clothes. I just got out of bed a few minutes ago." Then, not wanting to sound lazy, "I was up really late last night."

Abby was startled when Cash said, "What? Did you go swimming again?" But he must be joking, she told herself.

"Haha, very funny," she said wryly. She ran into the house to quickly brush her teeth, fix her hair, and change her clothes.

Cash

He wasn't joking about the swimming although he allowed her to believe he was. The night before, he had found himself in bed awake, reliving the events of the day. Abby being pushed into the water. His own dive off the bridge. Seeing her across the waves before she disappeared. His relief that she was okay. Jack pummeling Jeremy. Then there were the crows flying overhead and settling on the Sider property. It had been a crazy day. He laughed remembering Michael trying to scare off the crows.

After tossing and turning for over two hours, his mind buzzing with activity, Cash decided some fresh air might do him good. He crept outside careful not to wake anyone and walked towards the river. He didn't expect to see Abby when he arrived. It was the moonlight reflecting off her skin that caught his attention. There she stood, beside the river, completely naked. A second later, she dove head first into the frigid river.

Cash was startled. He'd never seen a woman naked. Not in real life anyway. And what was she doing in the water?

There was no turning back now. Hiding among the trees, Cash watched as Abby's head came up out of the water. Her face was spread into a grin from ear to ear. She let out a little squeal of delight, before leaning backwards into a somersault. But when her legs should have come up, Cash was astonished to see a fishtail. Abby's head came up again, then dipped under and disappeared. Cash watched curiously from the trees, scanning the water, waiting for her to reappear.

He heard a splash downriver. Carefully and quietly, he walked closer to the water for a better view. Just in time, he saw her head submerge and a tail come up to slap the water before disappearing again.

Cash was amazed. *Abby's a mermaid.* A thrill of excitement surged through him. "I think I've found the one," he mumbled quietly into the darkness.

He sniffed the air, enjoying her lingering scent on the wind before walking back home and falling into a blissful sleep.

Jack

It was loud, hot work. The earmuffs he wore muted the sound causing Jack to feel lulled by the rhythmic beat of the continuous hammering and high-pitched sound of the bench saw.

He didn't mind helping Dad in the shop. It was creative work building children's wooden toys. They'd gone out of style after the world became industrialized, producing plastic everything; but they were making a comeback with people who cared about the environment and sentimentalists.

Dad had a way with design. His concepts were simple and elegant, daring and bold, all at the same time. People loved his work.

Jack looked over at his dad working the saw. He was a man that no one understood. A man of contradictions – laid back but uptight, eminently practical but overwhelmingly emotional.

Jack kind of knew the feeling of that last one. He, too, struggled with controlling his emotions. That was why he beat up Jeremy Jones. That was why he couldn't eat certain foods. That was why he was beginning to understand his father. Dad bottled up his emotions until he was in a state of stasis, burrowing into himself and then lashing out towards the ones he loved most.

Jack was probably the only person who understood his father. He could see the value in bottling up his feelings. One could avoid a lot of unpleasantness, like fighter's remorse. Of course, if you bottle things up for too long, the resulting lash out is inevitable. *I mean, where is it supposed to go?* It's got to come out sometime.

He finished the piece he was working on and walked outside to get some fresh air. As he washed his hands from the hose, he looked up in time to see Abby disappearing around the corner with Cash McAllister. His body tensed as his first instinct was to run and catch up. He would make sure Cash didn't touch his sister.

Then he remembered Cash jumping into the river after Abby and realized that this romance was too far gone for him to stop it. "Chivalry's not dead," Jack chuckled to himself. It was one of his mom's favourite sayings.

Jack walked back into the workshop. "I just saw Abby walking with Cash McAllister," he said offhandedly to his dad. Michael turned around and looked at him.

"Which way did they go?" Michael asked.

"Towards the river."

Jack's father shook his head and grumbled under his breath about teenage boys. He turned to Jack and pointed out a few mistakes Jack had made on the dollhouse roof. He told Jack how to fix them.

Jack needed a break first. He bowed out claiming hunger and promised to bring Dad back some of Grandma Dianna's pie.

If it had been blueberry pie, Jack could have eaten it too but because it was apple pie, he didn't dare. For some reason, apples made him crazy. His mother had pointed it out to him. Countless times in the past, in the midst of a major meltdown, his mother came to him and said, "Jack, this is from the apple juice," or "Did you eat an apple today?"

It couldn't be denied. Apples had a bad effect on Jack. He often told people he hated apples and it was true. But the reason he hated them was not because of the taste. It was because he couldn't have them. He loved the taste of apples.

His diet restrictions were not confined to apples. He also had reactions to food dyes and preservatives.

When he was younger, Jack often rebelled against the diet restrictions hiding candy under his bed or accepting a muffin from the neighbour kid's mom. But Jack's reactions couldn't be hidden. Inevitably, he would begin to feel agitated and moody. Any little thing would set him off. It often culminated in a rush of anger that involved cursing, name-calling, and physical aggression. Mom used to hold him down in those moments to stop him from hurting himself or others. Dad would respond with punishment.

Eventually, Jack resigned himself to the diet restrictions preferring a level head to a boat-load of apologies later. Despite his careful eating habits, he still struggled with frustration and controlling his emotions. He had begun to perfect the stony face he'd seen on his dad so many times. If he couldn't control his reactions, he would not react at all. That was easier.

Jack glanced at the clock as he walked past the living room. Travis would be arriving any minute. Travis had a pattern. He'd get home from school, eat a snack, and change into his dirty clothes. Then he would head over to the Sider's on his quad to pick up Jack.

One thing Jack had not anticipated when he moved with his family to the Sider lands was that he'd make such a good friend in his cousin, Travis. They seemed to "get" each other. Things could be left unsaid in his company without misunderstandings taking place.

Jack was getting good on his borrowed quad. His antics would make his mother turn green if she ever saw him. He made sure to ride casually whenever he was in her presence. But when he and Travis were barreling over bushes, through creeks, and up steep inclines, Jack felt no compunction about disobeying the rules of safety.

Sure, he wore a helmet, but he did not moderate his enthusiasm for being challenged. Each time he overcame an obstacle and got the rush he was looking for; Travis would cheer him on. "What should we try next?" he would say excitedly. The two of them fed off each other's daring.

As he walked into the kitchen, his mother, grandmother and various aunts were talking about their favourite apple recipes. *Ugh, apples again,* thought Jack. He attempted to open the fridge but Grandma Dianna intercepted him. "What would you like, Honey?" she asked sweetly.

This is what Jack had hoped would happen. He gave her his most charming smile. "I came to get a piece of pie for Dad and make a sandwich for myself."

As she offered him a plate of sandwiches from the counter, she asked, "Are you sure you don't want some apple pie too?" Jack wished people wouldn't offer him apple anything. It was so hard to refuse.

"I can't," he said simply. He picked out the largest sandwich he could see, made on gluten free buns and filled with chicken breast, cheese, lettuce and mayonnaise.

"These are Sider farm apples, Jack," his mother suggested gently from her seat at the table. "You might not react to them." Jack was tempted to try to find out, but not today. The last thing he wanted to do was cry in front of Travis. If he got hurt or couldn't make a jump, he might not be able to control his emotions.

"Maybe some other time," he said. The women in the kitchen all stared at him. When they spoke again, they spent the next several minutes agreeing with Julea about

Sider farm apples and how they doubted Jack would react to them.

Jack began to feel angry. He didn't like it when people talked about him. He also wished everyone would stop talking about apples. He erupted. "I don't want any stupid apples ... OKAY?"

It worked. No one spoke as he left the room.

Michael

Having a bunch of women hanging around a kitchen was a luxury for Michael. Julea might be a nutritionist but she wasn't much of a cook. Grandma Dianna had a sweet tooth. She baked treats all day while the rest of the crazies chatted quietly in the kitchen. Michael didn't know what they had to talk about so much, but he wasn't interested either. He preferred to spend his days working anyhow.

Michael had realized long ago that Julea came from a family of tree-huggers on her mother's side and drug abusers on her father's side. There wasn't a normal person in the bunch and divorce ran rampant on both sides. They were mostly good people, Michael conceded, even some of the drug addicts. In fact, Michael got along better with Julea's wayward father than he did with her hippie mother. He'd always thought the tree-huggers were a little loony, to be honest.

Michael's family life growing up had been drastically different. His parents never separated, nor his grandparents or any of his aunts and uncles. He wouldn't say his life was easy but it wasn't chaotic like Julea's. She had moved around, gone to many different schools. Her parents divorced when she was 11 years old. Michael had lived in the same house for his entire childhood, then moved into a house on the same street when he left home. It wasn't that he had trouble with change. He just didn't see any reason for it.

It was a very big change moving to the Sider lands. But Michael was enjoying it. He loved the fresh country air. He loved the hard work to keep up the yard and gardens. He finally had leisure to pursue his passion. He had so many ideas and now he had the time and opportunity to make them come to life. Nothing motivated him like a new project did.

There were things he was concerned about though. Like the crows. He didn't know what to make of them. He hung onto a story Julea's mother had told him, hoping she was right. She said the same thing happened to a cousin of hers. The crows arrived en masse one day, then after awhile they just up and left again. She assured Michael that the crow issue was most likely temporary. It's hard not to believe something you want so badly to be true.

Michael also had concerns about Abby. She was growing into a beautiful, young woman. He knew that boys couldn't help but notice her. He also knew what teenage boys are like. Last week, all he had to worry about was a tame wolf. Now, it was Cash McAllister. Michael took his role seriously. He might not be the one she called "Dad" but he was the only dad she had.

When Jack returned with his pie, he couldn't help asking, "Has Abby been spending time with Cash then?"

Jack looked his dad in the eyes. "Well, he broke up with his girlfriend yesterday. And he dove into the water after Abby when she was pushed off the bridge. So, I'd say he's got the hots for her."

Michael grunted and looked away. He knew what teenage boys were after. It would take more than a dive into the water to impress Michael. He decided to keep a close eye on those two.

"Why don't you go down and hang out with your sister at the river," Michael suggested.

Jack laughed. "You think you're going to be able to stop their little romance?" He shook his head at his dad. "Good luck with that. It could be worse," he added. "Cash isn't such a bad guy."

Michael smiled back at his son. "Well, maybe you could go down to the river anyway. Just to say hi. Tell Abby I want to show her the dollhouse we're working on."

Jack shrugged and sighed. "Yeah, yeah. I'll go check on Abby. But I'm not hanging out with them. Travis is coming to get me."

Michael nodded his head once, squinted at the edge of the piece he was working on, then turned back to his work. "Tell Abby I want her to come back."

Jack sighed again. Then he walked to the river.

Julea

Her mother, aunts, and cousins showed up right after the crows. Word got around fast in the Sider family and five of Julea's closest matriarchs descended on the house with speed. In the years following, this would come to be known as The Meeting of Mothers.

They came because of the crows. At first, they kept their presence secret. It was their voices that Abby had heard in the kitchen that fateful day.

It seemed that their worst fears were realized. The End Days were upon them. But who was the Final Chosen One and who would be her Appointed Protector?

The allied forts shared information about who had received their powers that day. Including Abby, three young women made the change the same day that the crows came. It could be any one of them.

The mothers spent their days waiting for the news. Who would be the Final Chosen One? They wouldn't know until the crows left and the Appointed Protector was exposed. Conversation dwelt on where they'd gone wrong.

"If Abby could be the Chosen One, shouldn't we start preparing her?" asked Jessica, who was the youngest of them all.

"I'd really rather not," said Julea. "She will have the rest of her life to lead The Cause, if that is her destiny. Either way, I think she deserves a few months to enjoy her powers before she is burdened with The Knowledge."

The other mothers agreed. Although the circumstances seemed to scream for urgent action, the truth was that a few months would hardly make a difference and Abby could perfect the use of her powers in the meantime. There was nothing for them to do but wait.

"You will need to work with her," Grandma Dianna advised Julea. "Make sure she understands how to use all of her powers. She might love swimming but does she know about the singing?"

"She's been practicing her swimming at night when everyone else is asleep," Julea said. "I forgot about the singing. I'd better talk to her about that."

"Some of her powers will work in her human form as well," Julea's mother warned. "Singing may be one of them."

"It's true," realized Julea. "I will need to explain some of her more deadly powers to her as soon as possible." She glanced nervously out of the window at the workshop. She wouldn't want Michael or Jack to get hurt by accident. Abby wouldn't be able to live with herself if she hurt anyone in the family.

"Don't worry," Jessica assured her. "I gave Abby a copy of Matthew's book."

Abby

That week, while Abby was swimming nights and sleeping days, the mothers closeted in the kitchen baking and talking. Abby knew only that their discussions had something to do with the crows. But anytime she came near the kitchen, she was handed some food and shooed away.

She also noticed that her female relatives were paying special attention to her, giving her sly winks behind her brother and stepfather's backs. It obviously had to do with her getting her powers and keeping it secret, but Abby felt like there was something more. The way they watched her, as though they were assessing her in some way. She didn't know if she was passing the test but she didn't care. She had Cash McAllister.

By silent agreement, they were getting to know each other better. Cash came every day after school and picked Abby up at the house. Then they walked. They shared personal stories about hard moments in their lives. They talked about what they loved. They whispered secrets. Cash told Abby about breaking up with Mona and how bad he felt to hurt her feelings.

"Why did you break up with her?" Abby asked. She knew she was digging.

"I met someone else," Cash replied, holding her gaze for a moment. Abby turned away shyly.

They confessed their dreams, hopes, and fears. Cash made jokes. Abby giggled. But each day ended without a kiss. Abby wanted a kiss. It was the one thing that irritated her about Cash. He would blatantly declare his interest in her, but he wouldn't lean in for the kiss. Was he waiting for her to do it? Because that wasn't going to happen. That was the guy's job.

When it came time to go in for dinner, Abby and Cash would say goodbye and make a plan to meet again the next day. Abby would eat dinner with her family, ignore her stepfather's disapproving comments about Cash, then go up to her room and read "Water Warriors" until the house became silent. She counted it a blessing that her family members were early risers. It also meant they were early to bed. Bedtime was when Abby could practice her powers.

Unlike her other family members, Abby liked to stay up late. She preferred to do her creative work after dark, sleeping in or taking a midday nap when absolutely necessary. She usually spent her time drawing and writing graphic novels deep into the night. Lately she'd begun drawing herself in her mermaid form.

But the new late-night hobby that filled up most of Abby's time was swimming.

She had other powers, as well, that she learned about in her book. She could use her voice to lure people into the water by singing. She could control the movement and temperature of water. This all seemed unreal to Abby. In the book, the author suggested practicing your water control powers in a bathtub. He warned about the impacts on the environment when using water control powers. Abby was horrified at the degree of devastation she could cause if she didn't know better.

Abby was also curious about drowning people with her singing voice. It seemed unbelievable. She often caught herself singing without realizing it. Would she have to stop singing for the rest of her life? Abby loved to sing.

Matthew Collins suggested building a soundproof room to sing in. *How dismal,* thought Abby.

Abby poured over the pages of "Water Warriors," skipping the more boring chapters about the history of merfolk warfare, battle planning, and merfolk first aid. She would read them later. First, she wanted to know more about her powers.

She took many baths, quietly learning how to control water. At first, she sat in the tub while practicing. But the first time she froze the water, she realized her mistake. It took several minutes of teeth-chattering and shivering before she was calm enough to unfreeze the water again.

After that, Abby filled the tub but remained outside of it. To reduce water waste, she left the tub filled until someone needed to use it. That way she could practice on a whim anytime.

Abby wanted to test her singing powers badly, but the book warned that this power could inadvertently cause deaths. Collins advised waiting until all the other powers were fully formed before testing singing powers.

As far as Abby was concerned, life couldn't be better. She refused to think about returning to school next week when her blissful routine would have to change. Instead, she focused on the moments she had now to practice her powers and be with Cash.

On Thursday, as they parted ways, Cash told Abby he had something to show her the next day. Abby couldn't imagine what it might be. That night, as she swam in the moonlight, playing with different ways to move through the water, Abby was giddy with anticipation. What could Cash possibly have to show her?

Maybe it was the full moon. Or perhaps it was the nervous excitement Abby felt about Cash's surprise. Whatever it was, it intoxicated Abby. Feeling less cautious than usual, she decided to try one of her water-control powers in the river. She knew it had to be something small and simple so it wouldn't disrupt the entire ecosystem.

Abby focused only on the water that immediately surrounded her body. She could already swim very fast, breathe under water, and never get winded. But could she go even faster with a little help?

She thought back to her experiments in the bathtub. She'd been able to get the water moving in any direction and even create small waterspouts, which resembled tornadoes. Abby reasoned that if she urged the water surrounding her body to move a little faster, going with the river, it might give her a speed advantage. She ducked under. Using only the water around her body, she attempted to push herself forward. Because she was already moving slightly with the current, it took her a moment to be sure that her experiment was working. But yes, it was.

Abby smiled at a fish swimming near her. *This is so much fun.*

She spent the rest of the night practicing her new trick. First, she got used to it by moving forward with just the power of the water. Then she incorporated her arms and tail. In mere seconds, Abby resurfaced to see how far she'd come and didn't recognize her surroundings.

Now to get back home. She could swim against the current but it was time consuming. What if her water control technique worked in the opposite direction too? Sure enough, Abby travelled much faster when she manipulated the water directly surrounding her body. Within a few hours, Abby was able to go with and against the current at an incredible speed causing only a slight ripple around her body.

Shortly before sunrise, Abby returned from a trip downriver to find Grandma Dianna sitting patiently in the grass, eyes sparkling in the moonlight.

"Hi Grandma," Abby exclaimed. "How long have you been here?"

"Oh, just a few minutes," Grandma Dianna replied. "A helpful water sprite told me you weren't far."

Abby realized for the first time that there might be some truth to her mother's and grandmother's frequent references to magical creatures.

"Guess what I learned to do tonight, Grandma," Abby beamed as she bobbed in the water.

"What? Show me," replied her Grandmother with interest.

Abby spent the next half hour impressing Grandma Dianna with her swimming and water control tricks. They headed back to the house together before anyone awoke.

"Thanks for coming, Grandma," Abby said, as they walked hand-in-hand past what her mother called the Great Tree. It was the only tree on the Sider Lands that wasn't occupied by crows.

"Thank you for showing me your powers," Grandma replied. "I've always wondered what it would be like to be a mermaid."

"What is your supernatural form, Grandma?" Abby asked shyly. She wasn't sure if she was breaking some kind of etiquette by asking such a personal question.

Her grandmother giggled. "Well, actually, I'm a pixie. Want to see me change?"

Abby couldn't believe it. She'd only experienced her own change. She hadn't seen anyone else change yet. "Yes, oh please yes, show me," she said quickly.

"It might be hard to see in the dawn light, so watch closely." Before her eyes, Grandma Dianna disappeared. But wait, no, there she was. Or was she?

The tiny creature hovered in the air face level with Abby. As her eyes adjusted, Abby realized that it was indeed her grandmother. She was the size of her thumb, wings fluttering so swiftly that Abby could barely see them. Grandma Dianna slowly came closer until Abby could see her face. A tiny little Grandma fluttered above Abby's nose and smiled at her through the dawn haze. Abby blinked and there stood her life-sized human Grandma again.

"So, there really are pixies," Abby exclaimed.

"Yes, there are all kinds of pixies and nymphs and other interesting folks like us," replied Grandma Dianna. "They are everywhere but you won't see them unless they want to be seen. Just wait until the family reunion. You will be amazed."

Abby could hardly wait. Nine months till the family reunion. Her mother told her everything would change after that and to enjoy her powers in the meantime. Instinctively, Abby knew her mother was correct. She was a little curious. But there was a feeling of doom connected to her thoughts about "The Knowledge." Abby didn't want to know. Life was amazingly good and she didn't want anything to bring her down.

She could hardly sleep when she made it to her bed. In a few hours, Cash had something to show her. For some reason, Abby knew this would be a day she'd never forget.

Cash

Today was the day. He'd never shared his secret with anyone outside the family. But today he would tell Abby because she would understand. She was a mermaid, after all.

He couldn't concentrate on anything that morning. School was a waste, so he took to roaming the forest in the afternoon.

Cash knew Principal Logan would call his parents when he didn't return to class after lunch. Thankfully, Cash's parents always covered for him.

Angus often reminisced about the first year or two after he turned fourteen. He didn't spend much time at school either. Cash knew his father saw school as a diversion, not a necessary building block in life. Something to pass the time until Cash inherited the McAllister lands.

Having his future mapped out for him didn't upset Cash. It was a relief that he didn't have to make decisions about his future. He played the role to make his teachers happy. But there was very little he could get out of public school that would serve him in his destined vocation. No. His real school was in the real world. The forest.

Still, Angus was adamant that Cash learn proper etiquette in the straight world. That was what they called the world outside the forests. The McAllisters were human after all, so they needed to know how to get along in the straight world of humans. Living the way they did, the McAllisters often found the straight world to be a strange one indeed.

He didn't rush to the Sider's because he didn't want Michael to see him skipping school. He knew Abby was probably sleeping anyhow. He waited until school was over and arrived at the time he normally did.

Abby was sitting on the porch waiting.

Jack

As requested, Jack had followed Abby to the river that day and passed on his father's message to her.

"Tell him I'll look at it later," she said absently. She commanded Jack to leave with her eyes. It was an unspoken courtesy between them not to embarrass each other in front of the opposite sex. It took all of Jack's control but he resisted the impulse to tell Cash to keep his hands to himself. He walked off muttering to himself that he wasn't her personal messenger.

Instead of heading back to the house, Jack decided to explore the Sider lands until Travis got out of school. He and Travis had spent most of their time quadding through the bush on the McAllister property. It was more fun. Many paths had been laid down long before Jack or Travis arrived on the planet. The Sider lands, on the other hand, consisted mostly of orchard and untamed wilderness. Driving over the mounds between the rows was fun in some places but it got tired fast. The element of danger just wasn't there. Jack liked danger.

That day, however, Jack impulsively decided to walk into the orchard. Crows stared down at him from their perches. He grudgingly admitted he was getting used to them. Sometimes, he caught himself forgetting they were even there. Today they seemed to egg him on in a good way. Like they were happy to see him among the trees.

Care of the apple orchard was administered by Aunt Lacey's estate. Jack wasn't sure what it meant, only that his parents didn't have to pay for it. Uncle Duke, who was technically Mom's cousin, and his wife, Aunty Darla, took care of the apple trees. They lived in a small, circular dwelling in the center of the orchard. Jack had passed it a few times but out of respect for their privacy, he'd taken no more than a cursory glance. Today Jack wanted a closer look.

As he approached the cottage, or "the fort" as his mother called it, a strange feeling came over him. He felt a deep calm settling into his bones. A tingly feeling tickled his skin all over. He had the urge to smile silly. Shaking his head and chuckling, Jack looked around. He stopped suddenly.

There, in front of Jack, was the tallest, most climbable, most enticing tree Jack had ever seen. It stood singly in a sea of apple trees. How had he not noticed it before?

Jack's first impulse was to climb it. So, he did. He climbed up as high as he could. He was thrilled to find he could see most of the Sider lands and part of the McAllister property from his vantage point. He saw the big house, the barn and workshop, "the great tree" – another one of his mother's phrases.

He couldn't see the opening by the river where Abby and Cash sat, but he could see her red shirt through the trees. Below him was the fort, looking tiny from such a height. He could also see Travis coming down a path on his quad towards the bridge that connected the two properties.

Reluctantly, Jack began his descent. It didn't matter, he told himself. He would be right back. Travis had to see this tree. They would return and climb it together.

Abby

"So, what do you have to tell me?" Abby asked when they arrived at the river and sat in the grass.

"I have a lot of things to tell you," replied Cash. "For one thing, I want to say that I've really enjoyed hanging out with you this week."

Abby blushed. "Me too," she said.

"I also want to say that on Monday, when we're at school, I need to lay low a bit. I think it would hurt Mona to see me chasing another girl so soon after our break-up. I hope you understand…"

"Of course," interrupted Abby. "I think it's really honourable of you to think of her feelings. I wonder if there's anything about you that isn't wonderful." She smirked at him.

"Well, if there is, I'm not going to tell you," Cash laughed. "As long as you think I'm perfect, I might have a shot."

Abby didn't know what to say, so she giggled.

"Speaking of confessions," Cash drawled. Abby giggled again as there hadn't been any such discussion. Cash went on.

"I want to show you something. But before I do, I was wondering if you know about the treaty."

"What treaty?" Abby asked.

"It's an ancient agreement between your family and mine that requires my family to protect your land," Cash watched Abby carefully as he explained.

Abby had learned of many strange things lately, so she wasn't really surprised to learn about the treaty. But she was curious as to why the Sider lands needed to be protected.

"I'm probably not supposed to tell you this, if your family hasn't mentioned it," said Cash, "but I needed you to know about it so you'd understand what I'm going to show you."

"What are you McAllisters?" Abby teased. "Some kind of secret Ninja society or something?"

"Or something," Cash replied with a grin.

"Okay, hotshot," Abby encouraged. "Show me what you got."

Cash stood up beside Abby. When she started to rise too, he stopped her. "No, just sit there and watch. And don't be scared," he added.

Burning with curiosity, Abby leaned back on her hands and stared up at Cash. Gosh he was beautiful. Long, lean, muscular, handsome. All rugged and relaxed. I guess it's not going to be a kiss. Inwardly, she sighed.

Just when Abby started getting impatient, the air around Cash's body began to shimmer. Before her very eyes, Cash's face blurred for a moment before transforming into the face of a wolf. The rest of his body followed, also morphing into the form of a wolf. Standing before her was Abby's wolf. It only took her a moment to realize what this meant.

"You jerk," Abby snapped as she stood up, voice rising. "You've been hanging around me all this time pretending to be a wolf and it was you all along? And you didn't tell me?" She searched through her mind trying to recall if she'd ever said anything embarrassing to him.

Cash changed back quickly into his human form. He stood close to her, all solid and masculine smelling. Abby reminded herself she was angry with him.

"I wasn't allowed to tell you," he spoke urgently. "It is a family secret. But I had to tell you because… well, because…"

"Because why?" The fight had gone out of Abby. Of course, he couldn't tell her he was a wolf. Just like she couldn't tell him she was a mermaid. *Or could she?* As Abby considered it, she stared up at Cash. Indecision was written all over his face.

"I had to tell you because I think … we're meant to be together," he finished. "And I thought you should know."

In that moment, Abby melted. Her decision was made. She took his hand and turned towards the river. "I have something to show you too. But first you have to close your eyes."

Cash closed his eyes and Abby dove into the water. When she resurfaced, Cash still had his eyes closed. *Gosh, he's dependable,* Abby mused. "You can open your eyes now," she told him.

Duke

"Darla, take a look at that. Someone has wandered into the mirage and now we have a humungous tree in our back yard."

"Oh dear," said Darla, looking up at the boys climbing among the limbs of the monstrosity. "I think it's Julea's son up there. Should we pretend to be working?"

Duke rubbed his hands together and grinned. "No way," he said. "I'm going to have a little fun with them."

Jack

They spent the entire rest of the day up in the tree, watching the goings on of the people they loved. Countless wolves wandered through both properties. Jack hadn't realized how many were actually out there.

They watched Michael walk in and out of the workshop. They watched Aunty Jessica peeking out the window of the kitchen. They watched Duke and Darla puttering around their cottage.

At first, the boys spent their time pointing out animals and birds to each other. If someone down below moved, they might get poked fun at a bit. "Look at how my dad is walking. He's mad at something. I can tell by how he's walking," said Jack, hunching his shoulders in imitation.

"Are you sure he doesn't have to go to the bathroom?" asked Travis. The boys burst into laughter.

"What do you think of Abby and Cash?" Jack asked another time.

"I try not to," replied Travis, cracking up.

"But seriously," Jack pushed. "What kind of guy is he? Am I going to have to teach him some manners?"

Travis was quiet for a moment. "Nah," he said finally. "Cash is alright." He didn't elaborate so Jack let the subject drop.

Hanging out in the tree was a luxury. Sitting among the branches high above the ground, Jack felt safe and free. He was content to sit in partial sunshine, semi-reclined between two branches, and chew on a twig. One thing was for sure, he didn't expect much action down below.

Early Tuesday morning, while Travis was en route to school, Jack walked briskly to the tree. He planned to spend the day up there. He brought along a sandwich, a pear, and a small paper bag of gluten-free cookies.

He didn't notice anything out of the ordinary as he walked through the orchard. No one was milling about. In fact, if you didn't include the crows, he saw not a soul. So, when he was up moderately high in the tree and looked down to see three, pretty girls picking apples on the other side of the caretaker's cottage, he was more than a little surprised.

Jack had nothing better to do. He chose a branch with a view and watched them at their work.

He thought about climbing down and introducing himself but he didn't know what to say to them.

Their laughter tinkled up through the trees as they picked. Surprisingly, the crows vacated each tree that the girls worked on, returning to their perches when the pickers moved on to another. The girls alternated standing on ladders and gathering fallen apples from the ground.

Sweat glistened on their tanned arms. Jack was mesmerized by the cute way they bounced as they walked between the trees. He began to think of them as the cute, happy girls. For that was what they were. A hot morning, picking apples couldn't even get them down.

When Jack saw Travis coming across the bridge around four o'clock, he climbed down out of the tree to meet him. He carefully avoided the part of the orchard where he'd seen the girls working and intercepted Travis before he could disturb them accidentally.

"Come on and be quiet," Jack grinned as he spoke. The boys crept among the trees and the crows. When they reached the branch where Jack's pear still sat, Travis broke the silence.

"Why did we have to be quiet?" he asked.

"Shhh," warned Jack. "That's why." He pointed into the orchard and watched as Travis's gaze descended on the giggling, gorgeous girls below.

Travis's eyes popped open. He turned a warm grin back to Jack. "I see," he said. "Where did they come from?"

"I have no idea," replied Jack. "They were already working when I got here this morning. They've been picking apples all day. I guess Duke and Darla got them on the payroll."

Travis watched the girls for another few minutes, a thoughtful look on his face. He turned back to Jack with a mischievous glint in his eyes.

"Let's go down and introduce ourselves," he suggested.

Jack was nervous at the thought. "I don't know, man…" he began to decline.

"Come on," Travis persuaded. "Don't be a pussy."

Jack never backed down from a challenge. "Okay, I guess so," he said, as the thrill of adventure came over him.

Cute, Happy Girls

"Get ready, Gwen, 'cause here they come," said Ollie. Gwen and Mandy giggled in anticipation of Duke's plan.

Cash

He already knew what he would see when he opened his eyes. Abby was showing him her scales, *literally.* One day, when they were old and grey, he would tell her the truth and they would laugh about it together.

In the meantime, he hoped he could master a convincing expression of surprise.

"You can open your eyes now," she said. As his vision returned, he felt no need to fabricate his surprise. Seeing Abby in the water with her hair floating around her beautiful face and her chocolate brown eyes sparkling up at him; it was like walking into a brick wall. He felt the wind knocked out of him. He couldn't speak.

"Not only can I swim," Abby calmly explained. "But I too can change my form." With that, she sank swiftly under the water. Before Cash could anticipate her next move, a tail appeared where her head had been. In one flowing motion, it rose out of the water, and descended with a splash that soaked Cash's entire body.

As he wiped the water from his eyes, Abby's head reappeared above the surface of the river. "Well?" she asked excitedly. "What do you think?"

Cash felt happiness down to his toes as he answered her. "I think we're perfect for each other," he said.

Jack

It was the strangest thing. They had climbed down the tree and walked around the cottage to where the girls had most assuredly been working. But when they got there, they were nowhere to be seen. Quietly, the boys searched the surrounding area. They found no one. Certain that the girls were nearby, they whispered to each other.

"Let's climb the tree again and see where they went," suggested Travis.

"How did they move so fast?" Jack wondered.

"Maybe they went home," Travis replied.

It was easy to find their way back to the tree from any direction. It stood tall and imposing against the skyline. When they'd climbed high enough, they got a big surprise. The three girls were in the same spot as before. But instead of working hard picking apples, their three beautiful faces were turned up to the sky. As if they could see them clearly through the foliage, they were looking directly at Jack and Travis.

The boys were astonished.

"They know we're here? They must have hidden when we went down," reasoned Jack.

Travis waved at them. Sure enough, they grinned and waved back. "Let's go back down. We must have gone to the wrong spot," said Travis.

When they arrived at the spot where the girls had been working only moments ago, again there was no trace of them.

"How are they doing this?" Jack said exasperatedly. He did not like to be outwitted. Just to see what would happen, they climbed the tree again. Again, they saw the girls staring up at them from the same spot in the orchard as before. This time the girls giggled loudly as they waved up at the two boys.

Determined not to let them get away with playing him for a fool, Jack came up with a plan. "Okay, you climb down and walk to where they're picking and I'll watch what they do from up here," he told Travis.

"Sound plan," Travis concurred. Jack watched him climb down and make his way through the trees. It wasn't hard to see him. The rows between the trees were wide enough for a small tractor.

As Travis drew near to the girls, Jack switched his attention to them. They were back to their work, stopping for sips from their water bottles every so often. Jack realized they weren't going anywhere and waited for Travis to break into the clearing any moment. But to his amazement and utter frustration, Travis walked a clean circle around them. The worst part was Travis looked completely lost.

Jack kept pointing towards the girls. Travis seemed to understand, yet he would walk right around the girls again. He turned his head from side to side, looking in every direction, stopping and turning several times. But he didn't come upon the cute, happy girls.

After a few moments, he looked up at the tree in Jack's direction and shrugged. Then he started walking back towards Jack.

Jack was floored. What in the ever-loving world was Travis doing? When Travis returned to his perch, Jack was beside himself. "What were you doing? Are you blind?"

"What do you mean?" replied Travis. "They disappeared again. Didn't they?"

Jack shook his head. "This time, you stay up in the tree and I'll go down." He made his way back to the part of the orchard where the girls were picking. But when he got there, he found himself in the same predicament as Travis. He could not find the girls for the life of him. They were nowhere to be seen.

Something strange was definitely going on. Jack was going to find out what it was.

Jessica

Maybe if she stared at the crows long enough, she'd figure out the piece to the puzzle. She couldn't help it. She felt drawn again and again to the window. The crows stared right back at her like they were willing her to understand their message. But she didn't understand.

Her gaze drifted towards the sky and she blinked in surprise. "Um, Julea," she said uncertainly. "Why haven't

I ever noticed that massive tree growing up out of the middle of the orchard?"

"What tree?" Aunty Dianna and Aunty Jordana asked in unison, as they approached the window.

"That tree," Jessica pointed to the obnoxious sight. "It looks like it's been there for a hundred years or more."

Her mother giggled.

"What's so funny, Mother?" asked Jessica, a smile coming unbidden to her lips, as well. Julea, Aunty Dianna, Aunty Jordana, and Barbara also turned to Hannah, expectantly.

"Well, I visited with Duke and Darla last night and they told me that either Jack or Travis stumbled into the Great Desire Mirage. Apparently one of those boys loves tall trees."

"Jack," blurted Julea. "Jack loves to climb trees. He's probably up there right now."

"Well," Hannah went on, "he and Travis spent the afternoon up there yesterday and Duke said he was scheming up some tricks to play on them today."

Julea smiled. "Duke better be careful. He doesn't know Jack. My son is really good at figuring things out."

Jessica shook her head. "Well, all I can say is that boy has a big aura, so it's no wonder he has a big great desire too. I just hope he can contain himself; cause take a look at that tree. The boy done changed the landscape."

Aunty Dianna agreed. "I'm glad that it's so rare for people to stumble into that crazy mirage. It's been floating around here for too many years to count and only a few people have actually triggered it."

"Aunt Hannah, did Duke say what he was planning to do to the boys?" Julea asked Jessica's mother.

"Nope," she replied. "But I can just imagine." Jessica laughed with her female relatives. Soon she would give birth to a little one too. She rubbed her belly and smiled inwardly. *Hello little one. Can't wait to meet you. One day Uncle Duke will be playing tricks on you too.* She sighed with pleasure before turning back to the window to check on the crows.

Jack

Being the resourceful person he was, Jack quickly came up with a new plan. This plan involved homemade walkie-talkies. Travis helped him collect the parts from old telephones and an old radio. Michael provided the tools. In the space of a day, Jack had pieced together a functioning two-way radio for their covert operation.

By Thursday, the boys were ready. Jack's plan was simple. He would stay in the tree giving directions; Travis would be on the ground, taking directions. The directions would lead Travis straight to the elusive 'cute, happy girls.'

When Jack climbed the tree that morning, he half expected the girls to be gone. He was pleased to see that they were hard at work. The girls took turns resting and looking up at him in the tree. They smiled and waved. Jack grinned and waved back. He was enjoying their little game but he would be the last one to laugh. When Travis arrived after school, Jack met him at the bottom of the tree and sent him on his way. He climbed back to his perch and started giving directions.

"Okay, you're heading in the right direction," he encouraged. "When you get past the next tree, turn right." He watched as Travis followed his instructions. However, when he looked back at the girls, they were gone.

"Uh oh," Jack intoned over the radio. "They're hiding again." He scanned the orchard looking for movement. Travis' voice came back to him.

"Where should I go?"

"Walk up about four trees and turn right again," Jack replied. "That's where they were a minute ago." He watched Travis walk to the spot where the girls had been picking only moments before.

"There," Jack said. "You're right there now. But the girls are gone. Can you hear or see anything?"

Travis was quiet for a few moments. "No," he finally replied. "Nothing and no one."

Utterly disappointed, Jack resisted the urge to throw his walkie-talkie into the orchard below. He sighed. "Okay, I'll climb down. Let's comb the orchard on foot. Maybe we can surprise them if we're quiet enough."

There was no way Jack was going to let these girls get the better of him.

Abby

Abby climbed out of the water, and sat next to Cash in the sunshine hoping her clothes would dry out quickly. "It's risky changing in the middle of the day like this. I can't let my brother see me."

"He doesn't know about it?" Cash seemed surprised.

"I didn't know about it until it happened on Monday," Abby replied. "Apparently it's a family secret and we're not allowed to tell anyone under fourteen."

"So, you all turn into merfolk when you're fourteen?" Cash asked.

Abby laughed. "No, we all get different forms. What about you?" she asked. "When did you start changing?"

"Same as you," Cash replied. "Around the age of fourteen, we go through the change. But we don't keep it a secret from each other. The pups all know their fate. We just keep it a secret from the rest of the world."

"The pups?" Abby asked. "All of you become wolves?"

"Yes," replied Cash. "All of us except Travis. His dad and my dad are stepbrothers. They have different fathers. The rest of us grow up knowing that we'll become wolves when we hit puberty. It generally happens between the ages of thirteen and fifteen."

"No wonder our families are so close," Abby mused. "They have something in common unlike anyone else in the world."

"My dad says there are others like us. We are just one pack. But our main duty is to protect the Sider lands."

So many realizations rushed to Abby's mind. Cathryn talking about getting her "freedom" when she was fourteen. Travis shooing away Abby's wolf without fear. Abby's wolf. *Cash.*

"I got my powers from eating an apple from the Great Tree," Abby explained. "They are so delicious. Come on, you have to try one."

As they started walking, Cash reached out and linked his fingers with Abby's. The touch sent shocks of electricity through her body. Her skin tingled all over. Her heart skipped a beat or five. With effort, she controlled her breathing and smiled at him.

"Let's sit in the shade of the tree. At least no crows will poop on our heads," Abby said. "It's the only tree they've avoided."

The crows might be avoiding the Great Tree, thought Abby, but they sure seemed to be crowding around it. Was it possible that more crows had come or were they just congregating at this end of the orchard today?

Abby dragged Cash to sit on the ground beside her. "Okay, any time now," she said to the tree. The look on Cash's face when an apple dropped to the ground and rolled uphill to rest at Abby's feet was worth it. She picked it up, gave it a brief shine on her shirt and handed it to Cash.

He took a bite. Abby could see he was impressed. "You're absolutely right," he said. "This is the most delicious apple I have ever tasted in my life. Want a bite?" He held the apple to her mouth on the side he hadn't touched.

"Sure," said Abby before biting down. "Mmm, I need one for myself, I think." The tree dropped another apple, which rolled straight to Abby. She giggled. "Thanks a lot," she said to the tree. For several moments, Abby and Cash crunched away at their apples. Cash finished first and tossed his apple core into the orchard. A few minutes later, Abby did the same.

Abby spoke suddenly. "So, now what?"

"Now what what?" replied Cash.

"So, now we know each other's deepest secrets. Now what?" Abby knew she was pushing it. But she couldn't think of a better way to get her point across without coming out and saying it. And she was not going to come out and tell him to kiss her. He had to do it on his own so she could be sure that was what he really wanted to do.

"Um, I guess now we need to promise not to tell anyone our secrets and shake on it," he said. Abby groaned inwardly. Shaking hands was not kissing.

"Okay," she said. She held out her hand. "I, Abby Sider, promise to keep your secret until the day I die." When Cash took her hand in his, she experienced again that mind-blowing, heart-racing electricity that overtook her. She melted as Cash looked into her eyes.

"I, Cash McAllister, promise to keep your secret until the day I die," he said. But he did not let go of her hand. His eyes never left hers. He shifted closer to her. Abby could swear she had stopped breathing and time stood still. "I think maybe we could seal this deal a little easier with a kiss," he said as he leaned toward her.

Abby closed her eyes and parted her lips to receive him. *Finally!* her mind rejoiced.

Jack

Thursday was a waste. The girls were just too good at hiding. Jack felt like a fool. He was sure they were somewhere nearby watching him and Travis look for them. Friday, Jack worked with his dad during the morning and early afternoon.

"Where've you been all week?" Michael asked while they ate their lunch together in the shade of the barn.

"I've been climbing that tree," Jack pointed at the tree that grew up, up, up out of the middle of the orchard.

Michael shielded his eyes from the sun and stared towards the sky at the tree.

"It's funny because I never even noticed it until I practically walked into it on Monday," said Jack. "I don't know how I could have missed it. If I didn't know better, I'd think it just suddenly appeared."

"It's always been there," said Michael emphatically.

When Travis appeared around four, he had to wait for Jack to finish the piece he was working on. It was close to five when they finally left the shop. Jack climbed the tree as quietly and covertly as he could to see if the girls were still there. Sure enough, they worked in another part of the orchard, not far off the path to the river. He and Travis descended the tree. They split up intending to come at the girls from both sides.

Jack was busy checking around trees for places the girls might be hiding when Travis's voice interrupted his sneaking.

"You're never going to guess what I'm looking at right now," he whispered through the walkie-talkie.

"You found them?" Jack asked, disappointment rushing over him. He'd wanted to be the one to find them.

"No. I didn't find the apple pickers. But I almost got hit by a flying apple core. I followed the sound of voices and found your sister and Cash sitting under the Great

Tree holding hands," Travis chuckled. "I'm watching them right now."

"That better be all they're doing," grumbled Jack.

"Wait…wait…he's leaning in…it looks like he's going to kiss her…" Travis's voice trailed off and Jack waited for the verdict. *Dad's going to love this,* he mused sarcastically.

"Well?" demanded Jack. "Did he kiss her?"

"Yes!" Travis exclaimed. "Their lips are locked…" Suddenly, Travis's voice was drowned out by the flapping of thousands of wings and ear-piercing caws from the crows all around him. Jack ducked, instinctively covering his head with his arms. But the crows did not attack. They rose into the air above the orchard. Their collective screeches formed a cacophony of celebration.

As suddenly as they'd appeared, the crows lifted off into the sky. They blacked out the sun for several moments. Jack watched in astonishment as the crows dispersed, flying in every direction away from the orchard and across the sky.

Thrilled by the spectacle, Jack whooped into the radio, "They're gone! Those blasted crows are gone! I'm heading back to the house to see how my parents are taking it."

"That's a big ten-four," replied Travis. "I'll meet you there."

Julea

Jessica was at the window when it happened. She said there was no warning. The crows suddenly flew up into the air and departed. The noise alerted the rest of them and they crowded around the window in awe.

In those moments, Julea experienced a feeling of doom mixed with relief. Relieved that the crows were finally leaving, and Michael would be so happy. Doom because it was the beginning of The End. The Chosen One had found her Appointed Protector. The war would get much deadlier now.

"Well, at least we know it's not Abby," sighed Julea's mother. "It must have been one of the other girls. That doesn't mean that we won't have to fight just as hard, but…"

"How do we know that?" interrupted Aunty Hannah.

"Well, Abby's been home all week, right Julea?"

"Yes," Julea replied absently. She was still a little shocked by it all. She watched as the last of the crows disappeared into the distance.

"Where is Abby now?" Aunt Hannah asked.

At that moment, Jack's voice was heard through the window. "Mom! Mom!" he cried, as he raced towards the house. He burst in through the kitchen door. "The crows are gone!" Jack knew he was stating the obvious, but his mother would be happy to hear it again.

Julea turned to her son and opened her arms to him. "I know, Sweetie," she said as she hugged him tight. He returned the embrace and lifted her off the ground.

"And guess what else," he laughed as he put her down. "Abby kissed Cash McAllister."

Jack was the only one laughing. Julea watched as her son took in the faces of his female relatives. They looked back at him as though he'd just said someone died.

"What?" he said. "It's just a kiss."

Julea couldn't speak if she tried but she was saved from trying.

"What kiss?" said a deep, male voice from behind Jack. They all turned to see Michael entering the kitchen. Julea held back her tears. Somehow, she summoned a smile and found her voice.

"It appears that our daughter has fallen in love," she said to Michael. "Apparently, she kissed Cash McAllister."

Michael's face grew stormy. He turned to his son. "Go get Abby right now, please, and tell her to come home immediately."

Julea knew better than to try and reason with Michael in the heat of the moment. She just hoped he would calm down by the time Abby arrived. Because Julea knew something that Michael didn't.

Abby wasn't merely falling in love with Cash McAllister. Abby was the Final Chosen One and Cash was her Appointed Protector. Their relationship was the product of destiny, written in the stars since the beginning of time. Nothing Michael could say or do would change that. And with that thought, Julea burst into tears and went running out of the room.

PART THREE

REVELATIONS

Darkness shall remain until she who is Chosen
joins with her Appointed Protector.
In the moment of their joining,
thy last hope for salvation begins.

Jack

The following week, the crows were gone and so were the cute, happy girls. In fact, there wasn't anything cute or happy happening at all. The very air seemed desolate and brooding. Mom was different ever since the crows left. She seemed preoccupied and distant. It was very unlike her to keep so much to herself. Jack's Grandma Dianna, great aunts, and mom's cousins went home. Jack wished they'd stayed to cheer up his mom because the Creator knew he couldn't figure out what to do.

Dad was quieter than usual. And perpetually scowling. That one was easy to figure out. Ever since Michael had forbidden Abby to see Cash, she'd been lashing out at him. Interactions between them were tense and angry. Mom didn't even try to intervene. That was what worried Jack the most. His mother had always run interference between Dad and Abby. *Why not now?*

Since life around the house was so uncomfortable, Jack found it best to stay out of the house. These days he practically lived in the tall tree when he wasn't at school.

School had its own challenges. That little fight he had with Jeremy Jones hadn't won him any points at his new school. Kids generally greeted him with looks of fear, disgust, and a mixture of the two. Sure, there were some who still seemed to accept him, but Jack was all too conscious of the others. The ones who disapproved of him for what he did to Jeremy.

In retrospect, Jack admitted he'd gone too far booting Jeremy off the bridge. Even one shot to the head would probably have been enough. But "should haves" counted for nothing. Jack had earned his reputation and it would take awhile to undo it. In the meantime, he wore an emotionless mask as he endured the stares and glares.

As a condition of returning to school, Jack and Jeremy were required to apologize to each other. Jack would have preferred to get it over and done with Monday morning, but Jeremy's father wanted to be there. Because Mr. Jones was away on business, the "apology party" was postponed until Wednesday afternoon.

As Jack approached the office, he was surprised to see his Dad waiting for him. He must have looked confused because Michael enlightened him.

"Mrs. Logan told your mom that Jeremy's dad was coming," he said. "I thought I should be here too to make it even." Jack was speechless with relief. He'd been dreading the meeting with Jeremy and Jeremy Senior. For whatever reason, he felt much better entering the office with his own father by his side.

They were admitted to Mrs. Logan's office immediately. Jeremy and his father were already seated in the small room. They rose from their seats while Mrs. Logan made introductions.

Mr. Jones was a tall, imposing man with short, white hair and eyes so dark, Jack couldn't see his pupils. That in itself was disconcerting. But it was the first words out of his mouth that made Jack's insides freeze.

"I'm pleased to meet the young man who made a complete fool out of my son," Mr. Jones spat his words as he looked imperiously down at Jack. "I can only hope Jeremy will become half the fighter you have become, Jack *Sider*." Jack wasn't sure if the man was being sarcastic or serious. Unable to respond, he stood there staring at the man Jeremy called "Dad."

"His name is Jack Bagwell," Michael retorted. "I'm not sure what you're trying to say, Mr. Jones, but my son came here to apologize for a mistake he made. If his apology is not acceptable to you, then I don't see any reason to carry this conversation further."

Mr. Jones hadn't looked at Michael until that moment. His demeanor became conciliatory. "Ah, Mr. Bagwell. It seems that I, too, owe an apology to all of you. I am sorry for my awkward sense of humour. My wife scolds me often about it." He reached out to shake hands with Michael.

For the brief moment that their hands met, Jack watched as they stared each other down. Mrs. Logan thankfully spoke then.

"Well, I think it's time for the boys to express their apologies to each other, don't you, Gentlemen?" All eyes turned to her. "Jack, you go first."

Jack looked down at his hands and fidgeted self-consciously. "Look the man in the eye when you apologize," Michael instructed. Jack raised his eyes to Jeremy's. Jeremy was pale. He looked like he was going to throw up. *Okay, time to get this over with.*

He hadn't practiced what he would say. So, he said the first words that came into his head. "I was way out of line for what I did and I'm sorry."

Jeremy nodded and responded without encouragement from Mrs. Logan or his father. "I'm sorry too." Jack held out his hand for a curt handshake. They turned back to Mrs. Logan.

"Thank you, Jack and Jeremy. You may go back to class. Mr. Jones, Mr. Bagwell, thank you for attending." Mrs. Logan smiled her dismissal.

Not one to waste time talking, Jack's father nodded and walked out of the office with Jack. "See ya later," he said as he clapped Jack on the back. Jack watched as his father left the building.

When he turned around, he came face to chest with Mr. Jones. Looking up into those fathomless, black eyes, full of dark humour, Jack felt a chill run through him.

"We shall meet again, Jack *Sider,*" Mr. Jones said menacingly. But it was something much more frightening that froze Jack to the spot. As he spoke, Mr. Jones' lips did not move. A hideous grin never left his face as the words were spoken inside Jack's head. "When you've found your destiny, we shall most assuredly meet again," the voice growled ominously in Jack's mind. Then he turned and stalked off, leaving Jack shaken and confused.

Abby

It was all Jack's fault. If he hadn't told Michael about Cash kissing her, she wouldn't be in this position. Michael had unceremoniously banned Cash from the Sider property and grounded Abby.

It wouldn't have been so bad, if they could be together during the school day. But Cash wanted to spare Mona's feelings. So, Abby spent her school days pretending that nothing had happened between her and Cash. She held the secret in her heart; a deep treasure inside her soul.

The McAllister's all knew about the kiss. Travis couldn't keep his big mouth shut. So, Abby received messages through Cash's sister, Cathryn. Once, it was a folded paper with two words written inside. "Miss you." Another time, Cathryn simply said "Cash says hi."

The occasional glances they shared were charged and stomach-dropping. Abby lived for those glances. Brief moments in time when Cash's eyes locked on hers, and everything around her swam out of focus. It was so overwhelming that Abby sometimes worried it was the lack of sleep getting to her. Late night swims, little sleep, and emotional heartache combined to make her dizzy and light-headed.

Abby didn't invite Cash to the late-night swims, partly because she didn't know when or even if she would be going. Sometimes, she was too exhausted and fell asleep while waiting for the house to quiet. Sometimes she set her alarm for the middle of the night, but would wake up and change her mind, too tired to drag herself out of bed. But the main reason she didn't invite him was that she enjoyed the time alone to learn her powers. She didn't want to be distracted. She had so few hours to practice as it was.

After-school and during the evenings should have been Abby's time with Cash. Michael didn't have the right to keep her and Cash apart. She'd asked her mother to intervene. But Julea had looked at her with glassy eyes and told her to listen to her father.

"He's not my father!" Abby yelled, hoping Michael heard. "My dad wouldn't do this to me!"

Julea didn't respond. She turned her back and continued folding laundry. Abby ran to her room sobbing loudly.

Now Abby was barely speaking to her mother, although Julea didn't seem to notice. And towards Michael, Abby was hostile. If he wanted to mess with her life, then he would regret it.

It had been a week and a day since the crows left and Abby had been grounded and forbidden to see Cash. Even though it was daytime on a Saturday, and the behaviour was risky, Abby found a semi-hidden spot along the river and undressed on the bank. That was one thing about having underwater powers. When you changed back, your clothes were wet. Whenever possible, Abby preferred to take her clothes off first.

She needed a swim to clear her head. Making the change would cheer her up. She dove deeply into the water, smiling at the creatures below the surface that stared interestedly at her.

When Abby re-emerged, she was careful not to pop her head out. She rose until only her face was out of the water. Her body hovered just below the water line. She closed her eyes and floated there for a few moments enjoying the warmth of the sun on her nose and cheeks. So relaxed and unsuspecting was she, that when a voice broke into the quiet chatter of the forest, she nearly jumped out of her skin, making an awful splash. "Hello there," said the musical, female voice.

As Abby came to herself sputtering with a mouthful of water, she heard someone laughing. She scanned the shoreline and the air around her. It was a tinkling sound, like a wind chime under water, thought Abby.

"I'm sorry," came the voice again. "I didn't mean to startle you. I will come out of the water now. So, don't be afraid, okay?"

Abby looked down into the blue depths. She didn't see anything until a tiny, shimmering ball of fire came spinning out of the water. Abby lost her balance again, sinking into the river. This time she stayed under, collecting herself before rising carefully again to the surface.

As she slowly emerged face first from the water, Abby was startled to feel tiny little feet and hands clasp her nose. The touch felt natural and friendly somehow, so Abby didn't have the urge to swat a bug like she would normally do under such circumstances. Abby tried to focus on the shape in front of her nose. She felt herself going cross-eyed. The tinkling laughter fell around her again coming from the tiny creature. It detached from her nose and hovered above her face.

There, shimmering like hot metal in the sunshine, was a flying, fluttering little sprite.

"Hello Abby Sider," said the glittering, dark-haired creature.

"Hello," replied Abby.

"Don't worry, no one is nearby. I've posted lookouts along both sides of the river. I have a message for you to give to your mother," she said.

"My mother? You know my mother?"

"Yes, we are very close. But she has been avoiding me lately, so I need you to give her a message for me. *Oops!* I'm sorry, I haven't even introduced myself. People call me *Cookies*. I've been friends with your mother for many years." She held out her tiny hand to shake. Abby reached up with one finger and 'shook hands.'

"I'm not really talking to my mom right now," said Abby.

"Why not?" asked Cookies.

"My stepdad grounded me and banned my boyfriend from the property. And my mom didn't even stand up for me. I really, really miss him," Abby replied. It sounded silly even to her own ears. She was a little embarrassed.

But Cookies didn't scold her. She listened attentively, nodding her head and clucking in agreement. "I see," she said. "Yes, I can see why you're upset. Tell me, Abby, what were Michael's exact words when he forbade you to see Cash?"

For some reason, Abby wasn't surprised that this small creature knew all of their names. Not much surprised her these days. "Well, first he said that I was too young to have a boyfriend. Then he said I was grounded and Cash isn't allowed on our property."

"Were those his exact words?" asked Cookies.

"His exact words were 'I do not want that boy on this property again.' I'll never get to see him." Abby blinked back tears as her heart tore at the thought.

"Mmmhmm," replied Cookies. "Well, he said something about a boy, but he didn't say anything about a wolf." Cookies smiled conspiratorially at her. A small, glowing ember of hope began to burn inside of Abby.

Cookies interrupted her thoughts. "Okay Sweetie, I am going to share a little secret with you and I want you to tell your mama these exact words. 'Project Dark Angel is active.' Now, that's just between you, me, and your mama. Can you remember all that for me, Abby?"

"Yes," replied Abby. "I won't forget."

"Thank you, Honey Buns!" tinkled Cookies. She put two fingers in her mouth and blew a high-pitched whistle that could have been a bird's song. Another glimmering creature came flying from the Sider shore of the river. "I'm finished here!" Cookies sang to him. "Post guards around this section of the river so Abby can practice her powers during the day. She's looking tired. No doubt from all those late-night swims." The fellow nodded and flew away.

"You can practice safely here from now on, My Dear," Cookies said to Abby. "And give your mom a hug for me. If you ever need me, come to the water and call my name. I'll be here."

Before Abby could so much as wave goodbye, Cookies did three swift flips and shot back down into the water beneath her. Abby scanned the shores on either side looking for the little creatures who were supposedly protecting her while she swam. She couldn't see them, but she knew in her heart they were there. She smiled in all directions to let them know she appreciated the gesture.

Then she lowered herself into the river depths to frolic with the fish.

Michael

As he looked around his workshop, Michael found it difficult to muster the energy to work on any of his existing projects. He needed something new to get his mind off his deteriorating family. Abby pretty much hated him. Jack spent all his time in a tree. And Julea seemed to have had the life squeezed out of her. He felt himself getting angry just thinking about it. *What was wrong with that woman?*

At first, Michael thought she was mad at him for intending to punish Abby. That was Julea's usual reaction when Michael disciplined their daughter. She said he was too hard on her, that he needed to be gentler with Abby because she didn't trust his love. She said it was a stepchild thing that he wouldn't understand.

Michael had followed Julea to their room, ready to do battle with his reasons for keeping Abby and Cash apart.

"As Abby's father, I should be able to make decisions about when she's old enough to have a boyfriend," Michael began. But the soft sound of Julea's voice stopped him. "Pardon me?"

"I said go ahead," replied Julea. She was lying on the bed looking up at him. Her face was oddly expressionless. Only the glossy sheen of her eyes showed that she'd been crying.

"Well, what are you crying about then?" he asked.

"My baby girl is growing up so fast," Julea whispered, clearly trying to hold back her tears. This seemed a bit of an overreaction, but women were a mystery to Michael. Julea covered her face with her hands.

"Okay," he said, wishing to make himself scarce from such emotional, female nonsense. "I'll let you be alone then." Thankfully he knew that his wife preferred to be alone when she was upset. It suited them both and was one of the things that made their marriage work.

Julea turned away from Michael with her hands still covering her face. "Please turn off the light," she said to the opposite wall. Michael turned off the light and left the room.

That was a week ago and she was still strangely quiet and somber. Michael found the behaviour irritating. To give them both space, he'd focused on his work. Today he needed inspiration. What might he build?

A knock on the open door brought Michael out of his reverie. He looked up to find Frank McAllister standing there.

"Hi Frank," he said to Angus' older brother. Michael wondered what he was doing here. Was it something to do with Cash? He steeled himself for an argument.

"Hey Mike," replied Frank. He stepped into the workshop and held up a piece of wood from Michael's scrap pile outside. "I was wondering if you might be interested in selling some of your scraps," he said.

Michael breathed a sigh of relief. "It's not for sale," he said. "It's for free if you'll get it out of here for me." He smiled at his neighbour.

Frank smiled back at him. "What have you got there?" he asked Michael pointing to an unfinished toy.

They spent the next hour talking about the best woods and tools for their crafts. It was just the distraction that Michael needed.

Julea

Perhaps she should have been honoured or excited that her very own daughter was the Final Chosen One. But try as she did to muster up a positive reaction to the news, it wasn't there. Julea contemplated dangerous missions, the weight of the world literally on her daughter's shoulders, and other despairing thoughts that left her feeling cold and ill. To cope with her overwhelming fear for her daughter's future, Julea isolated herself from everyone. She needed time to process everything.

Michael would not know the truth about her family until the reunion. In the meantime, she needed to keep her feelings and fears to herself. She thought about talking to a friend, but she couldn't bring herself to say the words aloud. So, she isolated herself from everyone, hoping no one would speak to her about her daughter's destiny.

She was lost in thought cleaning the kitchen when Abby arrived with the message that would change everything. It had been delivered to her daughter by one of Julea's oldest and dearest friends — Cookies, the water sprite.

"Mom, did you hear what I said," whispered Abby. *"Project Dark Angel is active.* What does that mean, Mama?"

Julea was stunned. For the moment, she could barely breathe, never mind talk. She took in air in short little gasps as she gripped the kitchen counter and stared into her daughter's face. Could it be true? But of course, the message came from Cookies, so it must be.

Abby looked startled. "What's the matter, Mama? Are you okay? What does the message mean?"

Julea took a deep breath and pulled herself together. Unicorns can't lie but they can withhold information. Realizing she had no reason to keep the truth from Abby, she steeled herself and spoke.

"It means that they found your Aunt Lacey. It means that my sister is alive."

Abby

Everything was working out so well that Abby couldn't help but be nice to Michael. He was trying to be a good dad, after all. She was nice but not too nice, because she didn't want to tip him off what was really going on under his nose. Truthfully, she did feel a little guilty too. So maybe her good attitude towards her stepfather wasn't all goodwill. Abby had never disobeyed her parents before. And even though "that boy" hadn't set his foot on the Sider property at all; "that wolf" had been spending every afternoon in Abby's arms.

It felt too wonderful to resist. Cash was all too willing to play his part in the deception. Abby was in love and nothing could stand in her way.

The other wonderful thing was Julea. Learning that Aunt Lacey was alive had brought her mom back to life. Abby wasn't sure why she'd been moping around so much over the last week, but it relieved her to see her mother back to her energetic and happy self. Abby did as she was told and kept the news about Aunty Lacey to herself. She sensed that something was happening that she knew nothing about and it excited her. Abby was especially honoured that her mother had entrusted her with the meaning of the coded message Cookies had given her. Life seemed wonderful again.

In a couple of weeks, she and Cash wouldn't need to hide their relationship at school anymore and everything would get even better. She resisted the urge to whistle while she walked down to the river to meet her wolf. She wasn't sure if whistling was the same as singing. *Hmmm,* something she would have to look up in her "Water Warriors" book.

JUNE 2009

Jack

The school year was ending. Jack looked forward to spending his days swimming, quadding, and climbing his tree. The Bagwell-Sider's had survived their first winter in Beaverdell, and it had been a success. Mom spent the months getting her herb shed organized for spring. Dad built a fire almost every night in the fireplace. Abby spent most of her free time at the river with that tame wolf.

The snow hadn't stopped Jack from climbing the tree often. He felt protected from the rest of the world up there. Not that he needed protecting. He felt safe and apart. Being a bit of a loner, he liked it that way. He didn't spend too much time alone anyhow. Travis joined him every day.

It was the last day of school. Since it was a half-day, both boys convinced their parents to let them skip-out. They slept late, met after breakfast, then made their way to a nice spot high up in the tree.

"Only a couple of weeks until our birthdays," commented Travis once they were settled in.

"Yeah, my mom is freaking out," laughed Jack. "I catch her talking to herself all the time. Reunion this. Reunion that. Dad is hiding in the shop permanently."

Travis also laughed. "Yeah, my dad doesn't say much about it. But I can tell he's hiding something. It better be good or else I'm going to be really disappointed."

The boys grew quiet, retreating into their own thoughts for a few moments. Then Jack spoke.

"I know it's none of my business, but I've been wondering about something for a long time. And since we know each other pretty well now, I think you won't be offended if I ask you."

"What's that?" replied Travis.

"I was at your mom's funeral but you and your dad weren't there," said Jack tentatively. "Why not?"

Travis was quiet for a few moments before he answered. He wouldn't look Jack in the eye. "My dad says my mom isn't dead," he replied. "He says why would we go to a funeral for someone who isn't dead."

"My mom doesn't think she's dead either. But how can your dad know for sure?" Jack pressed.

"I don't know," said Travis. "He doesn't say much else. Just that my mom isn't dead and someday she'll be back."

He paused and Jack sensed he was going to say more, so he stayed silent, waiting.

When Travis spoke again, he was quiet, as though someone might hear what he was saying even though he was high up in a tree, far from any other person. "I don't know if he's right or not. Part of me wants to believe that it's true. But, if she is alive, then why isn't she here? What kind of mother abandons her own son like that? Part of me thinks that maybe it would be better if she was dead. At least it's a good reason for being gone so long."

Jack didn't know what to say. He didn't say anything. After a few moments, he pointed at his sister walking through the orchard with her pet wolf. "Sometimes I think my sister is in love with that wolf. One day she's going to marry it and get in the local paper for being a crazy wolf lady."

The thought obviously cheered Travis and he smiled in return. "Your sister is definitely in love with that wolf," he said knowingly. "Let's go throw apples at him and see what your sister does."

Jack laughed uproariously. "Okay, but if we get in trouble, I'm blaming you."

Abby

Months had passed without anything changing. But change was coming like a hurricane. Abby could feel it in her bones.

As the family reunion approached, Abby's excitement rose. It was an alarming kind of excitement. Dread and anticipation in equal measures. She did not speak of her growing fears to her mother or Cash. It felt too private, *too personal,* to share with anyone. Abby's instincts told her to keep her own counsel.

At night, she had a recurring dream that Cookies the sprite came to her while swimming; much like the first and only time they'd met. In the dream, Cookies had a message for Abby instead of her mother. The words were spoken in that singsong voice like it was coming from under water. Shivers ran over Abby every time she remembered them: "You must be strong, Abby. You are our greatest hope. *We believe in you.*"

The words echoed in her mind. Repeating themselves over-and-over like the dream repeated itself every night. She was both haunted and caressed by it and looked forward to the recurring dream with as much fervor as she dreaded it.

It had been nine months since Abby and Cash officially became a couple. At school, they spent every free moment together. Cash was a grade ahead of Abby, but they organized their schedules for second term so that they could spend their spares together.

Most evenings and weekends, Abby spent time with Cash in his wolf form. Michael knew they were seeing each other at school. But he would not bend at home. Cash was not allowed on the property, so they continued their subterfuge. Cash was Cash whether he was in his wolf form or his human form. Over time they began to understand each other in a very unique way.

Even though Cash could not speak human language in his wolf form, he could understand it. Still, Abby relied more on gestures and facial expressions to communicate with Cash, rather than actual speaking, when he was in his wolf form. The conversation should have been limited. But most of the time Abby felt like she knew what Cash was thinking. He also seemed to know what she was thinking. One day they discussed it.

"It's like we are speaking to each other with our minds," Abby whispered in the lunchroom amid the chatter of the other students.

"Maybe it's because I'm a wolf," Cash replied quietly. "When we're in our wolf forms, we can communicate with each other telepathically."

"That's so cool," said Abby. "I hope that's what we're doing." But there was a part of her that worried about Cash reading her thoughts.

Cash looked her in the eyes. "Try it right now," he whispered.

Abby stared back into his eyes and projected an unusual thought. It had to be something totally random to see if it really worked.

Cash laughed, completely caught off guard. "You think I'd look good in women's underwear? Wow. I had no idea you were into that kind of thing."

Abby wasn't sure if it was funny. "Read my mind and find out if I really am into that kind of thing," she said playfully. Cash stared into her eyes hard for a long time.

"I'm not getting anything. Want to throw me a bone?"

Abby smiled, relieved that her thoughts weren't an open book to Cash. *Only in pink underwear,* she projected. *Any other colour would look funny.*

Cash laughed again. "It's not going to happen, Abby. I will say I'm glad it's your voice I hear in my mind rather than seeing pictures."

Abby giggled. After that, they didn't spend much time talking aloud.

Julea

It wasn't until her brothers arrived two days before the rest of the family that Julea felt like she could breathe again. They gathered at the fort to share their gratitude and grief that Lacey was alive yet not out of danger. The three of them sat at a cozy, circular stone table, lit in the center by a single candle. To give them space, Duke and Darla took their dog, Bosco, for a walk.

Julea could tell that Rik was agitated. One hand moved constantly as though it was grasping for something that wasn't there alternating with his other hand which tapped spastically on the tabletop. Teej sat with relaxed shoulders projecting a calm demeanor but his eyes were serious and deadly. It was Rik who spoke first once they were alone.

"I've been there," he said. "I sat outside and watched the house. They knew I was there too. He knew I was there. But he did nothing to stop me."

"How did they know you were there?" Teej asked.

"I hung a pink bandana from a branch of the tree I sat in," Rik replied. Julea wasn't sure if he was joking.

"That's so dangerous, Rik," Julea pleaded. "Remember what he did to you last time?" A movie reel of images flashed through Julea's mind. She hadn't been there, but her imagination was horrible in itself. Rik being dragged through the streets behind a car, submerged under water repeatedly, burned, stabbed, doused in chemicals, and beaten within an inch of his life.

"Of course, I remember," he snapped. "I still dream about it every night since I quit those God-forsaken sleeping pills. But I can't stand by and do nothing. Lacey must know we are there waiting for our chance to get her."

"Yeah, I'm with Rik. Let's go in and get her out." Teej spoke with calm confidence.

"It's easier said than done, as you know," replied Julea. "You said so yourself, Rik. Jerematicus knew you were watching him. He doesn't seem concerned which indicates he is more than ready for an attack at any moment. This lack of concern is what scares me the most. Perhaps this is a trap. The information was leaked quite suddenly and conveniently."

"The Elders are not moving on this," urged Teej. "If they don't do something soon, it may be too late. It's already been nine months since we found her. We are lucky she's survived this long."

"We have to trust that the Elders know what they're doing," Julea reasoned. She was met with silence. "We have to trust that there is a reason why Lacey's rescue has been delayed," she said desperately.

"There is only one reason that I can think of, and you both know what I'm talking about," Rik sneered. "The Elders are not in a hurry to rescue Lacey because the Drenykin are afraid of the curse. Only a fool would kill her. But that doesn't mean they can't torture her."

"Or bleed her little-by-little, keeping her alive but weak, and using her blood for their warriors," Julea whispered.

"I'm haunted by these things too," Teej insisted. "I'll follow your lead, Rik. Tell me what you think we should do. My talons are itching to shed some Drenykin blood. I just have to stop myself from ripping off their heads with my teeth. They taste disgusting." Rik chuckled.

"I agree this has gone on long enough," added Julea quietly. She couldn't bear to imagine what Lacey was enduring at the hands of the Drenykin. Especially this particular Drenykin.

"Alright," said Rik. "I've got a plan in mind but there's one thing I'm not sure you're going to like about it, Julea. We're going to need Abby."

"But Abby doesn't even have The Knowledge yet," Julea replied incredulously.

"Calm down, Julea. We won't go until after the Fires of the Elders," Rik replied. "Don't you think it would be better if her first mission was with us by her side?"

"Don't worry, Sis," assured Teej. "We won't let anything happen to her."

"Plus, if we do get into trouble, the Elders will have no choice but to help us," Rik added. "They won't risk losing the Final Chosen One."

Julea was silent. She didn't like the idea of using her daughter as an insurance policy for a deadly mission. But Rik's arguments were convincing and Lacey only had so much blood to give. "I guess you're right," she said to her brother.

JULY 2009

Jack

As the extended and obscure family members poured in, the Sider property became a mass of colourful tents and hammocks. Jack was introduced to too many people to count. At each introduction, there was a phrase used to describe Jack that he was unfamiliar with. He was embarrassed to ask what it was since everyone seemed to know the word well and find it very interesting.

At first, he thought they were saying "green tea" and considered it odd. Once he realized it was "tree" they were saying, he assumed they were referring to his love of climbing trees (and the fact that he spent all his spare time in one) and left it at that. He made a mental note to ask Mom about it later.

A large, joint birthday party for Travis and Jack was held in the barn. The decorations were beyond imagination. Jack spent much of the afternoon looking at various ribbon or light designs wondering how someone could have made them. Intricate, colourful, *fascinating* designs.

Jack did not know most of the people in attendance. But they knew him. He was showered with attention and congratulations for turning fourteen and reaching his "Sacred Summer." Travis was surrounded by his McAllister family members, which left Jack with the crazy Siders.

One of his more interesting relatives was his mom's brother, Rik. He was all of five foot four, covered in tattoos, with a loud laugh, and a tendency to do back flips on a moment's notice.

"Ahhh, Jack," he said walking purposefully towards Jack shortly after he arrived. "Happy birthday, Birthday Boy. I hear you're a Green Tree, but not to worry, we'll fix that for you soon enough. Hey Teej, bring over some of that apple pie for my man, Jack, here."

"Um, no thanks," replied Jack. He was a bit intimidated by Uncle Rik.

"You don't like apple pie?" Rik asked. "Okay, okay, well how about some apple custard? Hey Teej, forget the pie, bring the custard!"

Jack scrambled for something to say that would distract Uncle Rik from the apple desserts. "Uncle Rik," he said quickly. "I have something to ask you."

It worked. Rik's attention was focused on Jack's question now, rather than his appetite. "What? What do you want to ask me? You can ask me anything. Go ahead." Rik waited impatiently, the fingers of his hand playing an invisible piano on his leg.

Jack had to think of something fast. He looked down at the ground. *That was it!* "Umm, I wanted to ask you…" he paused hoping the question wasn't offensive, "…umm, why are you wearing hot-pink nail polish on your toes?"

"Oh!" Rik's laughter boomed through the campground. "Well, there's a simple answer to that question. Hot pink is my favourite colour!"

Jack didn't think that really answered his question and he wasn't sure what was so funny, but Uncle Rik's laughter was contagious. Several people in the general vicinity laughed along with him, including Jack. Uncle Teej put his arm around Jack's shoulders.

"Hey Jack. Happy birthday. Here's an apple. Rik said you're hungry," Teej handed Jack an apple.

"No, I didn't say he's hungry," corrected Rik. "I said he's a Green Tree." Rik broke into laughter again.

Teej chuckled. "Even better," he said. "I'll bet it's something good."

More confused than ever, Jack nodded his head, apple in hand. He was glad for the interruption when Duke walked up and greeted them.

"Hey," he said. "You talking about Jack being a Green Tree?"

"Yeah," said Teej. "I bet it's something good."

Duke nodded. "You're probably right," he agreed. He turned to Jack. "Are you confused?" Jack couldn't think of a reason to lie, so he nodded. "It's okay," assured Dave. "They're just having a little fun with you. It's not supposed to make sense to you." Jack felt a little better but his curiosity was definitely piqued.

"What's a Green Tree?" he asked his uncle.

"It's kind of hard to explain but you'll understand after the Fire of the Elders," Duke replied. "On a completely different note, there are some people I'd like you to meet."

Jack hadn't heard of the Fire of the Elders. But his uncle was already walking away. "Okay," he said. He followed Duke towards the orchard but stopped short when he saw them. It was the cute, happy girls. They were decorating an apple tree on the edge of the yard, smiling and giggling like he remembered them.

Duke stopped beside him. "These are your cousin, Lyll's, friends. They said they wanted to meet you," he said.

The three girls stopped what they were doing and turned their eyes to Jack.

"Hi Jack," said the blonde-haired one.

"Happy birthday, Jack," the three girls said in unison. They giggled.

Jack smiled back at them. "Hi," he said. The girls walked over and each in turn, greeted him with a hug.

"Jack, this is Mandy, Gwen, and Ollie. Girls, this is Jack."

"We know who he is, Duke," said Ollie, the dark-haired one with blue eyes. "He's the tree guy."

"He's Abby's little brother," said Gwen, the dark-skinned girl with large brown eyes.

"You've met my sister?" Jack asked politely.

"No," replied Gwen. "But we'd like to."

"Well, I can introduce you," Jack offered.

"Oh, yes, thank you!" The girls spoke in unison again. Jack scanned the yard, looking for his sister. He suspected she was down by the river with that wolf as usual.

"Maybe when she's around," said Mandy. "We'll be right here. By this tree we're decorating."

"We promise," they said together, then giggled again.

Jack wasn't so sure he'd be able to find them again, but he promised to try. He was about to excuse himself when he remembered that he was still holding the apple that Uncle Teej had given him. "Would any of you like an apple?" he asked the cute, happy girls.

All three of them shook their heads vigorously.

"Oh no, you must eat it," Gwen pushed.

Rather than argue, Jack smiled and excused himself. He would leave the apple in the tree for Travis to eat later.

Travis

Travis was suspicious. "Why'd you bring me an apple?" he asked Jack from his favourite branch.

"I thought you liked apples."

"I do, but everyone down there keeps saying I'm green tea and offering me apples. I've eaten three since yesterday already."

"It's 'Green Tree'," replied Jack. "They're doing the same thing to me. I assume it's an inside joke of some kind in reference to us hanging out in this tree all the time. Ollie called me 'the tree guy' too."

"Who's Ollie?" asked Travis.

Jack sat up suddenly and smiled. "I almost forgot to tell you," he said. "I met the cute, happy girls. Uncle Duke introduced me."

Travis could still see the three girls from last summer quite clearly in his mind. "How could you forget to tell me that?"

"I know where to find them again. They want to meet Abby. I'll take you by tomorrow too, if you want."

"Sure, if you can really find them again," Travis teased with sincerity. He and Jack had miserably failed in their previous attempts to find the cute, happy girls. He reached into his pocket and pulled out the small wooden image he'd carved earlier for Jack. "Here, I made you something." He tossed the trinket to Jack confidently.

Jack's reflexes were smooth and he caught the small gift easily. "What's this? I didn't know you could carve."

Travis felt warm all over to see the admiration in Jack's eyes. "Neither did I," he replied. "I was hanging around with my dad and I did it. This is my first piece."

Jack stared down at the wooden replica of the gargantuan tree the two boys climbed almost daily. "This is really, really good. Are you sure this is your first time?" Jack was clearly skeptical.

"Hey, I'm just as surprised as you," Travis assured him. "You should have seen my dad's face. He was floored. He couldn't stop looking at it and examining it, shaking his head like he couldn't believe it." Travis smiled at the memory. He was sure his father had never been so proud as he was that day.

Travis was feeling great. It started when he woke up. He'd felt different. He'd grown up knowing he wouldn't become a wolf when he was of age because his dad, Frank, was Angus' half-brother by another father. Frank had been adopted by Angus' father, but he had not inherited what could only be passed by blood: the ability to become a wolf. Yet, today, when so many pack members had congregated, circling the Sider property in service to the treaty, Travis felt wolfish.

He'd gone outside to eat with some of the pack members. Many were in their human forms, plates full of bacon and eggs from Janine's kitchen. Many more roamed near the house as wolves. One of them was especially familiar to Travis.

"Hey Cash!" he yelled. Cash looked back and trotted towards him. When he was near enough to speak without yelling, Travis asked, "Want to go for a walk?"

Cash nodded. They began to walk into the woods. Cash stopped for a moment and phased back into his human form. "Happy birthday, Trav! Nervous about your party?"

"Uh, maybe a little. There are going to be a lot of people I don't know there," he replied. "But I think I'm just feeling the energy of the pack. How's the guarding of the Sider reunion going?"

"Pretty quiet," replied Cash. "Our ancestors had most of the fun. But Dad says things are going to get real serious real soon, so enjoy the peace while it lasts. Lately he's been riding me hard to sharpen my skills. He says I have an important role to play. I have no idea what he's talking about and I wish he'd stop saying it." Cash smiled.

Travis laughed. "Yeah, well, good luck with your wish. I've never seen Uncle Angus be deterred from a course. If he thinks you're the messiah, I'll take his word for it and start praying to your laundry pile."

Cash began to smile but was distracted, cocking his head to one side. "Look out!" he yelled suddenly. But his voice turned to a growl as he phased into his wolf form. Travis didn't have time to react. One moment a black blur was hurtling towards him and the next he was rolling on the ground, a mouthful of fur and the taste of blood dripping into his throat. He released whatever he was biting into and jumped back.

"Travis!" It was Cash's voice but it seemed to come from inside his head. He looked up at the great, grey wolf form of Cash.

"What happened?" he asked. His voice came out garbled and fuzzy.

"You killed it! It's a Drenykin hellhound! I can't believe he got this far into the compound," Cash was beside himself. He whimpered worriedly.

"I killed a ... a ... what?" Again, the words did not come out but echoed in his head with Cash's voice.

"Travis! You're a wolf!" Cash's words startled him. *What was he saying?* "You're a wolf! You're a wolf! How'd you do it? I thought you couldn't do it!" Cash's voice rattled inside Travis's skull. When the words finally sank in, Travis looked down at his body. He was a wolf indeed.

Cash changed back into his human form. Travis slowly felt his wolf form dissolving too. They stood over the hound. It was a massive, black beast. Its head, alone, was the size of a large pumpkin. Fanged teeth showed around the animal's curled back lips. His pink tongue protruded, matching the bloody wound where Travis had bitten out his throat.

"What did you call it?" Travis asked.

"It's a hellhound," Cash explained. "You'll be trained now that you're one of us. They'll teach you everything you need to know. I've chased a few with the pack, but I've never seen one up close or dead. We have to report this right away."

And so it was that Travis had started his day as a wolf. A short time later, he went to his dad's shop to tell him the news. When Frank asked him to make the change, he couldn't do it. But Travis was sure that once he was trained, it would be no problem. Cash made it look easy.

While visiting with his dad, he suddenly had an inspiration to carve the tree. He picked up his dad's tools and went right to work on it.

Now, sitting in the tree with Jack, munching the apple, Travis felt content. It was the only word to describe it. Content. He leaned back against a branch and sighed a happy sigh. Then he begged Jack to tell him more about the cute, happy girls.

Angus

"This is serious business. That hound was very close to our house. We need to get these lazy puppies to pay better attention. Call a meeting for midnight. We'll do it telepathically. Everyone stays at their posts. One speaker at a time," Angus instructed his son.

"Yes, sir," Cash replied. "I will pass the word. And father, I just want to say that I am ashamed I didn't sense the hound sooner. Travis could be dead right now and it would be all my fault."

"Not your fault," Angus corrected. "It is the fault of the entire pack when one of our enemies gets that close to us. The thing I don't understand is why he attacked Travis. If he'd had others with him or if Travis posed a great danger, I could understand. But he sacrificed his life in an effort to kill Travis."

"Maybe he was simply closer to Travis when he attacked," Cash suggested.

"Perhaps," Angus replied. "But here's another theory. Hellhounds are trained to immediately kill any Fatum they come upon that has immense powers. Like us, hellhounds can sense how powerful those are that they meet. When they meet a very powerful enemy, they are instructed to act immediately. The element of surprise is surprisingly effective."

"But Travis isn't Fatum," Cash replied slowly. "Well, I guess he is Lacey's son and he did turn fourteen today ..."

Angus nodded and smiled. "Well, we know he has developed our powers. Perhaps being raised with wolves affected what kind of Fatum form he would be gifted with. Perhaps the combination makes him extra powerful ..."

Angus didn't know the answers. All he knew was Travis never could stay out of trouble. It occurred now to Angus that all this time it was trouble that found Travis, rather than the other way around.

Abby

Abby was startled awake by a sound. It was pitch black. Before she could wonder what had awoken her, she became aware of a deep, wracking pain in her belly. It radiated through her entire body culminating in one searing hot spot on each of her wrists. She attempted to hold her stomach, but her arms were bound to what felt like a large, wooden chair.

"The Sacred One stirs," came a snide, cruel voice from the darkness. Abby jerked her face in the direction of the masculine voice but could see nothing. She realized her eyes were covered by some kind of thick material reeking of men's cologne.

"Who are you?" She tried to scream but her voice came out in a hoarse, painful whisper. She couldn't summon any saliva to ease the sensation. She searched frantically in her mind for how she came to be here. Her last memories were of lying in bed holding the wolf figurine gift from Cash to her chest.

"She must be delirious," the voice spoke again. "Take off her blindfold and get her some water. I don't want her cursed death on my hands. Let her die on someone else's watch."

"Yes, Jerematicus," said a voice at her ear. She felt the blindfold come off and blinked as a blast of light tore at her vision. The scene around her seemed to fold in and out. She saw doubles, triples, then brief glimpses of one man. He stood in front of her smiling, *with his hair on fire.*

"Hello, my dear," he whispered as he leaned in close. Smells assaulted her – whiskey, cigar smoke, cologne, garlic, and perspiration.

As he drew nearer, Abby realized that his hair wasn't on fire after all. It was pure white giving the illusion he was a human matchstick. Long, skinny, and bobbing in and out of focus.

"What do you want with me?" she begged. Her plea was interrupted as water was suddenly sloshed into her mouth. She choked and sputtered it down, relishing the pain it caused. So, this is how something can hurt so good.

"Tsk tsk tsk, don't you worry, little one. It will all be over soon," replied the matchstick man. He swung something in his right hand. Strung on a leather strip was a wooden object carved in the shape of a unicorn.

Abby felt like crying but no tears would come. Water sloshed down her throat again. She moved her face under the deluge hoping to get a hold of herself to think straight. It worked a bit. She could take in her surroundings.

She was bound to a chair in the center of a small room. There was one closed door, a desk and a few chairs scattered around the room. Three people were in the room with her. The matchstick man. The one who had taken off her blindfold and given her water. And another that was out of her field of vision. Abby could sense her. A woman standing behind her, not speaking. Three, massive, black dogs lounged on the floor near the door.

Abby appealed to the woman. "Please help me," she whispered. "Please help me." No other words would form. Abby looked down at her arms. In addition to the binds that held her, bright red tubes stretched out from each of her wrists. The tubes came together at a point ending in a bag, which hung from a pole. Drip, drip, drip. As Abby focused on the dripping, she realized it was blood. *Her blood.* They were draining her blood.

Abby swooned. Her last thoughts before falling into unconsciousness were: *"I'm sorry, Mom."*

Dianna

"Okay, so we have to do this strategically," she instructed the others. "Jack must not go another day without eating the sacred fruit. The Fire of the Elders is tomorrow!"

"We can't let him catch on to what we're doing, Mom. If he thinks we're hiding something from him, he'll disappear into that tree and we'll never get him down again," replied Julea.

"If he gets suspicious, we switch to Plan B," Dianna calmly replied.

"What is Plan B?" whispered Billie Jean.

"Plan B, we tell him the truth."

The mothers that huddled in the kitchen shook their heads sadly, then bent to their task with determination.

Jack

The day started out pretty normal. Jack grabbed a blueberry croissant out of the fridge. His favourite fruit. While toasting it, Abby offered him some of her yoghurt smoothie. He turned it down, but threw a few croissants and slice of lemon meringue pie into a knapsack.

Grandma Dianna watched him closely but to Jack's relief, she did not offer him an apple. Instead, she rushed him out of the kitchen. "Get yourself outside and have some fun," she said.

"Okay, okay," replied Jack. "Abby, do you want to come with me? There's these girls that want to meet you for some reason."

"Okay," smiled Abby. As she passed Grandma Dianna, they high-fived and giggled.

Jack ignored them. He walked out of the kitchen with Abby close behind.

Abby

Under normal circumstances, Abby would never have agreed to babysit Jack all day, following him around and climbing trees. But knowing he would get his powers that day made it very exciting. She hoped the excitement might distract her from the horrible nightmare she had last night.

It seemed so real. Abby could still smell the musky cologne and something else. Something so horrible that Abby could only think of it as the stench of evil. Was it the smell of blood? She recalled the carved wooden unicorn that swung back and forth from the matchstick man's hand. One defined object in a room spinning with confusion and pain.

Whatever it was, Abby told herself it was just a dream and turned her focus to the day ahead.

Grandma Dianna had explained that three requirements had to be met for Jack to receive his powers. First Jack had to eat an apple from the Great Tree. The mothers worked diligently in the kitchen the night before, mincing and pureeing apples so they could hide them in the blueberry croissants. They also made sure that every other food available in the kitchen had the apple ingredient hidden in it somehow. If Jack ate anything in that kitchen, he would be eating apple from the Great Tree.

Abby was concerned that Jack would be able to taste it, but Grandma Dianna shook her head. "I told it to hide its flavour," she said. Abby was skeptical.

The second requirement was that Jack could not know he was going to receive his powers. This was important but Grandma Dianna didn't explain why. She only said, "Others have had The Knowledge first and it came at a great price."

The third requirement was that Jack would have to have an emotional experience strong enough to make his powers appear spontaneously. When Abby had fallen into the river, she had been terrified. She thought she was going to die. It was a strong emotional experience.

Abby's job today was to make sure Jack ate the food from the kitchen and encourage him to have a strong emotional experience. This was going to be fun. For once she could get Jack back for all the times he'd played jokes on her and scared her. And she wouldn't even get in trouble for it.

"Why are you smiling like that?" Jack interrupted her thoughts.

"Oh, no reason," she replied. "I'm just in a good mood. By the way, can you show me your tree today? I haven't been up there yet." Abby had ready-made reasons to hang around with him all day.

"Sure," Jack said with some surprise. "I remember you used to love climbing trees with me."

"Yeah, I guess I've kind of grown out of it," replied Abby. "But I really want to check out your tree today. It's so tall. It looks like you can get really high up."

"I'm meeting Travis there after this," Jack told her. "I promised these girls I'd introduce you to them. Travis wanted to come but he can meet them later."

"Who are these girls? Are they your girlfriends?" Abby drawled the last part to be clear that she was teasing.

"No, but they're cute," Jack shrugged and smiled.

Hmmm, this might be more difficult than I realized, surmised Abby. He's not the sensitive little boy he once was. Her mind whirled with ideas as she waited for a new opportunity to make Jack mad.

Jack

Jack had no problem finding the tree they'd been decorating the day before, but the cute, happy girls were nowhere to be seen. His cousin Lyll saw him and ran over.

"Mandy, Ollie, and Gwen went into town," she informed Jack and Abby. "They'll be back later. What are you guys doing?"

Jack considered it for a moment. "We're going to the tree," he said, nodding towards it.

"Can I come?" Lyll asked.

"Sure," Jack replied.

"Why didn't you move here with your parents, Lyll?" Abby asked as they walked.

"It's a temporary posting and I didn't want to leave my school," Lyll replied.

"What do you mean by a temporary posting?" Jack asked.

"Oh, well, I guess posting isn't the right word," Lyll scrambled for an explanation. "Um, they're just here until your mom and dad hire someone else," she explained.

"Oh, I didn't know that," said Jack. He had assumed the fort was Duke and Darla's permanent home. "Where do you go to school?"

"It's on an island off the coast," Lyll replied vaguely. "You'll probably hear about it soon. A lot of our, um, family members go there."

Jack thought that was strange. He hadn't heard about any boarding school. He hoped his parents didn't plan to send him there. Beaverdell High wasn't so great, but it was better than a boarding school on an island.

"You say you didn't want to leave?" Jack asked with surprise. "I can't imagine liking a school that I can't go home from."

"It's not that kind of school," Lyll replied. "It's...it's a special program for...gifted students."

Ahhh. Now Jack understood. Lyll is a smarty-pants. All he could think to say was, "Cool." They walked the rest of the way in silence. Jack climbed up first.

Just as he was getting above the tree line, an apple came flying out of nowhere and bounced off the side of his head.

"Ouch! That really hurt, Abby! I almost fell!"

"It wasn't me," she replied from below him. "It looked like it was thrown from the ground."

The grounds were filling up with relatives and obscure family friends. It could have been anyone. It could have been Travis. Jack let it go and continued his climb to his favourite perch high in the tree.

Abby and Lyll settled in around him as Travis arrived.

"Hey, did you throw an apple at us?" Jack asked immediately.

"No," replied Travis. He found a spot above Jack because Lyll was sitting in his usual place.

Abby giggled. "Someone threw an apple at us and it hit Jack. He almost fell out of the tree."

Jack ignored her comment. There was a time when he would have gotten mad if someone teased him. But he wasn't a child anymore. He could tolerate a little teasing.

"Is that right?" asked Travis. "Well, I wouldn't worry about it. I hear that all us Ryked kids have hard skulls."

Jack laughed. "You've been hanging around with Grandpa Torrents."

Travis smiled back. "Yep. I was on my way here and he was camping down by the river. As I went to walk past the clearing, I heard this voice say, 'Hey there, Buds, do you know where I can find some sweet leaf around here?'" Travis deepened his voice to imitate Grandpa Torrents' rough timbre. "I turned around to see this short, bearded man standing buck naked in front of me. The only thing he wore were some leather, fingerless gloves."

"Oh, my goodness," Abby groaned. "How embarrassing! Why must he walk around naked all the time?"

Jack laughed uproariously. "So, you stood around talking about how hard our skulls are?"

"No," replied Travis. "Just as I was telling him where to find sweet leaf, little Kade came running up from the river and did a sidelong dive head first into a tree. That's when Grandpa said not to worry because Ryked kids have hard skulls. Apparently, it runs in the family."

They all laughed. Grandpa Torrents was a legend in the family. Despite his strange affinity for nudity and rowdy nature, they all loved him dearly. Grandma Dianna had been married to him once, but his unfaithful, partying ways grew tiresome for her. She moved on and found herself a calm, decent man named Thom to spend her life with.

Jack liked Grandpa Torrents but he was more comfortable with Papa Thom. His thoughts were interrupted by Lyll.

"Little Kade is such a sweetheart. But why is he here? I had to wait till I was fourteen to come down."

"Mom said Kade is a special exception. I'm not sure why but I do know he spent the last few months in foster care. So maybe it's because he's finally home with his family and they want to make him feel safe again," replied Abby.

Everyone was quiet for a moment. Then Travis spoke.

"I was in foster care once," he said.

"You were?" Jack was surprised Travis had never mentioned it before.

"Yeah, three years ago, when my mom took me to the grocery store and left me there. I walked over to look at the magazines while she shopped. Usually she came to get me, but this time she never came. I wandered up and down the aisles and in and out of the store looking for her until the manager noticed me. Instead of calling my dad, he called the police. They put me in foster care. My dad had to jump through hoops to get me back. It took several months."

"That's terrible, Travis," said Abby. "Did you ever find out what happened to your mom or why she left you there?"

"No. That was the last time any of us saw her. She disappeared."

"Something must have happened," assured Abby. "No mother would ever abandon her child like that if there wasn't a good reason."

"I guess," said Travis.

Jack groped for something to say but found nothing. Conversation had been weird and depressing all day. He pulled four croissants out of his backpack and handed them out to the others. He took a large bite of his croissant.

"Yum," he said. "This is the best croissant I've ever tasted." He wasn't just trying to change the subject. It really was incredibly delicious. The sky suddenly looked bluer. He became aware of the birds chirping around him. He regretted having passed the croissants around. There was only one left in the bag.

"Want to eat mine, Jack?" asked Abby. "I ate a big breakfast." Jack nodded his head vigorously and took the croissant back from her. Finally, the day was getting better.

Samantha

It was her first reunion. Dad was giddy. He kept introducing her as his daughter, the Green Tree. But when she asked him what he meant, he just giggled. "Oh, you'll find out soon enough," he said.

Samantha was perched at his feet, reapplying a fresh coat of hot-pink nail polish to his toes. Her father sat still with his eyes closed. His head rested against a tree. It was rare to see him so still. Samantha knew her dad better than most people did, but he was a mystery at the same time. Something drove him that Samantha did not recognize or understand. She just knew he was driven. And that he was tortured by demons and nightmares.

Dad never spoke about the demons to Samantha but she'd heard him crying to her mother more than once. Sometimes he painted the beasts. Hideous creatures with blood dripping from their mouths and claws reaching out for you. Samantha would watch them burn in flames later. They were masterpieces but her father did not want them. He built bonfires out of them in the night.

"I cannot bear to look at them," he sobbed to his wife when he thought Samantha was sleeping. Now she stared up at him. Even at rest, his face was lined with anxiety and fatigue. She hoped she could help in her small way to brighten his day.

"There you go, Dad. I'm finished," she told him quietly. He opened his eyes and looked at her.

"How many apples have you eaten?" he asked.

"I've had five since we got here. One this morning. Why are you making me eat apples?"

He ignored her question. "You should be out getting into trouble or something," he said. "This is the last day, my little sweetie. Thanks for pampering your old dad, but it's time for you to run along. Go find your cousin, Jack. It's his last day too."

"Last day for what?" Samantha asked. But she didn't really expect him to tell her. Lately everything he said was a riddle.

"It's your last day to be a child, little darlin'," he said. "Go be a child and play." His serious tone made her feel tense. Then he smiled. "Just go have fun. Please." He begged kindly.

"Okay," Samantha replied. She followed her dad's gaze to the massive tree growing up out of the center of the orchard. "I'll go find Jack." She began to walk towards the tree. It was a beautiful day and the sun warmed her face as she walked in and out of the shade through the orchard.

As she approached the trunk of the giant tree, Sam heard loud, angry voices. One of them was Jack's. Suddenly there were loud cracking sounds like a snapping whip and breaking branches overhead. Samantha looked up in time to scream before flames engulfed her.

Jack

He'd hoped the good food would lighten the mood, but Abby couldn't leave well enough alone. Jack nearly jumped out of his skin with her next comment.

"Jack told me that you hope your mom is dead. Is that true, Travis?"

Travis glared at Jack. "You told your sister that?" he asked.

Jack was flabbergasted. How could Abby say that? She'd never betrayed him before. He stuttered. "Uh, I, uh…"

"Oops, I guess I shouldn't have said that," Abby jumped in. "Sorry, Jack. Sorry, Travis."

"I never said I wished my mom was dead," Travis said heatedly. "That's not what I said."

"I'm sorry," said Jack. "I don't think I used those exact words either. We were talking about Aunt Lacey…"

"Oh Jack, you don't have to be so sorry," interrupted Abby. "Travis has told me your secrets before too."

"What?" Jack and Travis both yelled at the same time.

"Yeah, remember, Travis? You told me it was Jack who was throwing apples at Ca ... my wolf."

"I never said that," Travis said emphatically.

Now it was Jack's turn to be mad. "That was your idea!" He yelled at Travis. "You were throwing them too!"

"At least I didn't call your sister a crazy wolf lady," accused Travis. This was too much. Jack could feel his skin beginning to prickle like it did right before he lost his temper. He took a deep breath trying to control himself but it was too late. He watched as the rest of his croissant left his hand with force. It flew through the air towards Travis and hit him in the face.

For a moment, it looked like Travis was going to be calm about the whole thing. He used his sleeve to wipe his face, sprinkling crumbs onto his shirt and smearing a streak of blueberry across his cheek. Then he lunged.

Jack didn't have time to brace himself. It occurred to him that he would break many bones by the time he hit bottom, as he fell backwards off his perch. He flailed his arms trying to grip something. He was aware of only one thing. The sound of breaking branches.

Something wasn't right. Jack realized he should be falling faster. Something large and black came in and out of his vision on both sides. There was an ear-piercing scream from below. Jack looked down to see his cousin, Samantha, directly in his path.

"Look out!" He tried to scream but instead his face became filled with fire. He instinctively pulled away and that is when it happened. The great black things that had been thrashing and crashing around him snapped into sync with each other and Jack's body lifted effortlessly into the sky. He let out a screech of triumph as his entire body rose in electrical ecstasy.

Jack didn't know what was happening. He only knew that he had suddenly grown these massive, magnificent, snapping wings. He hovered in the sky, looking down at his red-and-black scales and reptilian body, trying to understand. Before he could make sense of his transformation, a new sound caught his attention.

Flapping clumsily into the air below him was a huge dragon the size of a house! The creature was all black, covered in scales … just like Jack's scales! Was Jack a dragon too?

The creature rising up into the sky blew flames, snorted, and stumbled through the air towards Jack. Confused and scared, Jack tried to back away and again, he found himself trying to scream. But no scream came out. This time, Jack saw the flames coming out of his mouth. Or was it more aptly called a snout? He looked down in disbelief at his body. *I'm a dragon.* Distracted by his changed form, Jack was unprepared for the jolt when the other dragon barreled into him.

Neither of them seemed able to regain their balance, as they awkwardly flapped their wings and breathed flames of fear and disorientation.

Down out of the sky they tumbled towards the ground. Down, down out of the sky as the Earth Mother spun towards them. Their bodies crashed to the ground taking out the barn and a large tent.

That was all Jack remembered when he woke up later that day.

Rik

Nothing could have prepared him for the news about his daughter. He expected her to get powers. Yes. What might she have been if she hadn't been bathed in fire that morning? A pixie, like Lyll? A dragon, like Jack? A queer elf, like me? He smiled through his tears. It wasn't Sam's destiny to assume her natural form, whatever it might have been.

But he was proud of her. She was already a legend.

Jack

"Oh, my goodness, Jack. It was spectacular. First, you turned into a dragon, and then Travis turned into a dragon and he comes stumbling towards you up in the sky. And you're just looking down at yourself and totally don't see it coming!" Abby vibrated with laughter and excitement.

"I'm a dragon?" Jack asked in wonder. But he already knew the answer. *He was a dragon.*

"And then, WHAM, Travis flies right into you, and you both fall out of the sky and squash the entire barn and Uncle Rob's tent while you're at it! Luckily Kade was still at the river with Grandpa Torrents."

"I'm a dragon," Jack said again more certainly. Then giggled. He couldn't seem to say anything else at the moment and it amused him.

"Yes! You're a dragon! And guess what? I'm a mermaid! I've been waiting so long to tell you. That day when Jeremy Jones pushed me off the bridge, I turned into a mermaid!"

Jack's head began to spin.

"And you know what else, Jack?" Abby went on excitedly. "Lyll says it was probably the Great Tree that threw that apple at you. She says the Tree is known to get angry sometimes and he, it, or whatever has perfect aim!"

Jack blinked uncomfortably. It was too much information all at once.

"Jack."

He turned to the sound of his name on his mother's lips. She stood in the doorway.

"Mom, did you see me?" he asked.

"Yes, Bub, I saw you. You were amazing and beautiful."

"Is this real, Mom?"

"Yes, Baby, it's real."

"What's happening? I don't understand…"

"I'm sorry I couldn't tell you before but you'll understand everything very soon. Tonight, at the Fire of the Elders, Grandma Rose will explain everything. Rest right now because you took a hard fall. And you were unconscious for a while which worries me."

"Because Travis LANDED on you!" Abby bellowed excitedly. Jack began to feel woozy. Her voice wasn't helping.

"Abby."

"Yes, Jack? Are you cold? Do you need a pillow? Do want something to drink?"

"Can you please go away?"

"Um, okay," Abby smiled before walking out the door. "I'll see you later around the fire. And Jack…I love you."

"I love you too, Abby. Now, please go away."

Rose

The Ode would be more difficult than usual to tell. Many of her own great-grandchildren were being initiated this year. Then there was little Kade with his premature powers. It was enough to break an old Fatum's heart. Steeling herself for strength, Rose Ryked looked around the fire at the familiar and unfamiliar faces of her comrades. This bunch would serve during the End Times. This generation would decide the fate of the world and all its inhabitants.

There was Abby, looking so innocent and happy. What would The Knowledge do to her, the Chosen One? In a few years, what would Jack be like? A weather-beaten, war-hero like his grandfather, Torrents?

It had grown quiet around the fire. They were waiting for her to begin. She asked herself, must I begin? *Is there no alternative to this life of war and pain?*

"Hey Mom, can you get this party started? I'm going to have to go for a whizz pretty soon," Torrents cajoled her. Quiet laughter erupted around her. It was light-hearted but she caught his drift. It was a silly attempt to bring her out of her melancholy. He was such a dear son.

"Yes, Torry, I'm almost ready to begin," she replied with a loving smile. "Has everyone found a comfortable seat? Make sure that all the new recruits are up front so they don't miss anything."

"We're all here, Grandma Rose," sang Abby.

"Oh, you are, are you?" Rose chuckled. "Alright then. I suppose I'd better begin."

Cash

He stood on the outskirts of the gathering, speaking quietly with his father. The Fire of the Elders was about to begin but Cash's curiosity about Travis made it difficult for him to pay attention.

"You have to listen to the Matriarch," Angus instructed him exasperatedly. "I've told you that you are going to play a very important role in The Cause. You must not only have The Knowledge, but you must live it in your soul. I don't want you to miss a word."

"I won't," replied Cash absently. "But Dad, what happened with Travis? Yesterday, he was one of us, a part of the pack. Today he is a dragon. I don't understand."

"Julea says he's an empath," replied Angus. "She says that he takes on the powers of others when he is in their presence. Even humans. Whatever their skills or talents are, Travis inherits them in their presence."

"That's incredible," Cash said as he pondered the meaning of it.

"Yes, it's incredible and very rare," Angus agreed. "Now, go sit with Abby and pay attention."

Rose

She began at the beginning. "At one time, we were one race. We were called the Fair Folk and we had the Creator's favour. Our duty, as Fair Folk, is to care for the human spirit. We are capable of appearing identical to humans so that we might live among them undetected."

"And so, we can flirt with them," added Torrents with a wink.

"Yes," agreed Rose, chuckling. "You might call us the external conscience of humankind. We use our powers discreetly and subtly to teach humans lessons and point them in the right direction. For instance, we orchestrate coincidences. The Creator instructs us only to nudge humans; allow them to find truth for themselves. But we must never interfere with free will."

"As we observed the increasing destruction of the Earth Mother by humans over time, despite our gentle prodding and best efforts, some of us became disillusioned." Rose paused. She raised her voice to be sure that she was heard. "There were some among us who thought that the restriction on interfering with free will was a mistake. They began to speak out against humans, calling for their destruction. Impassioned speeches and the irrefutable evidence of the Mother being destroyed by human callousness persuaded many more to reject our duty to the Creator.

"There was a revolt. A rebellion that damned us all for eternity. We became fractured and split into two groups. Those of us who continued in service to our Creator became the Fatum. Those who turned away from our service, in preference of waging war against humans, became the Drenykin.

"The Fair Folk had, at this time, always been joined with our totems. Without them, we would die. We live only as long as our totems live."

"What do you mean by totems, Grandma?" Abby asked.

"Our totems are the plants, animals, and waterways that we are joined to. Most of you — our half-breed offspring descended from both Fair Folk and humans — you are free like humans."

"I'm a pure-blood Fatum," Cookies the Sprite explained. "I am joined to my totem. The river that runs alongside this land to be exact. If Beaverdell River was to dry up, I would die along with it."

"Did you choose that river?" Abby asked.

Grandma Rose answered her. "Oh no. Pure-blood Fatum are chosen by our totems. They choose us for the light and colour of our souls."

"That is why you'll see Drenykin tied to weeds and deadly waterfalls and such. Their souls are blacker than the darkest nights," added Teej.

"But who are the Drenykin?" asked Jack. "Are they demons? Are they half-human, like many of us?"

"No dear," Rose corrected. "Let me explain. You see, over time, our physical similarities with humans resulted in many interspecies relations between Fatum and humans. Descendants of such a match were born into our mutual, human-like form without powers, or so we thought at first. As we all now know, mixed-blood Fatum get their powers sometime around their 14th summer after they've eaten from the Great Tree.

"The Great Tree is not just one tree here on our land. There are Great Trees in other communes all over the world. Where there is a mixed-blood Fatum, there is always a Great Tree nearby."

"Communes?" asked Travis. "Are there others like us?"

"Yes," Grandma Rose answered. "The Fatum are every-where. We blend among humans. I quite think most of the time, we forget that we're not." She giggled and the children around her giggled too.

"Drenykin, on the other hand, would never lower themselves to mate with humans. All Drenykin are pre-sumed to be pure-bloods. That is not to say it doesn't happen. If it becomes known that a Drenykin offspring is a half-breed, the commune will kill the child and banish the deceitful parent. But I digress.

"Shortly after the Fair Folk became two races and split into the Fatum and the Drenykin, we were all visited by a strange but powerful dream. The dream prophesied the end of the world as we know it here on Mother Earth."

"What was the prophecy?" Travis asked impatiently.

"In our dreams, the Creator told us that the Earth Mother is declining because of human disregard. We were told our purpose is to save the Mother from destruction by humankind. And this purpose was called 'The Cause.'" Rose responded gravely.

"But what does this have to do with us now? I mean, this happened hundreds of years ago," Travis said.

"Because if we fail, the Earth Mother will die and with it, every living thing. Including us."

Silence filled the air around the crackling fire. Rose waited for the truth to settle in their hearts, then went on.

"After this message was delivered, the Drenykin had a resurgence. They became more determined than ever to put a stop to humanity's destruction of the Earth Mother. They also became more determined than ever to put a stop to us."

"But if we have the same goal, the same Cause, then why do the Drenykin wage war against us?" Cash questioned.

"Our goal is the same. But the path to achieve that goal is disputed. The Fatum seek to heal the broken spirits and bodies of humans, knowing that the healing of the Earth Mother will naturally follow. The Drenykin, on the other hand, seek to rid the Earth Mother of humankind by poisoning their food supply among other things. Once the population is small enough to manage, the Drenykin plan to finish them off in cold-blooded murder. They might have left us out of it if we hadn't started mating with humans. But to the Drenykin, we deserve to die like the humans we've loved just for the act of loving them."

Rose paused and took a sip of water. She had never doubted herself for loving a human. Their children were perfect and that was all that mattered to her. It was a hard life they were born to. She continued the story.

"So, in our human form, we are activists, advocates, and yes, like Michael says, we are tree-huggers." She smiled at Julea's blushing husband. "For some of us, tree-hugger is a literal description." Laughter erupted momentarily among the older generations. Rose smiled, then turned serious.

"In our interactions with humans, we are subtle and discreet with our powers. But we can be dangerous. Our supernatural powers are our weapons of war against the Drenykin. We are a peaceful race but we are forced to defend ourselves and humans. So, we must."

"But how did the McAllisters come to be involved?" Abby asked. "They aren't Fatum, are they? I mean, they're all wolves."

"Thank you. I was just getting to that. It was around the same time, that a select group of humans were also visited in their dreams. These humans were summoned to volunteer for The Cause. The humans who had the dream were able to see through the shield created by the Great Tree. They came to us, as instructed, and offered to protect us. The McAllisters are descendants of those volunteers. They roam Mother Earth as both human and wolf, acquiring the ability to change forms at will when they reach maturity. Communes all over the world have treaties with their wolf protectors."

"Do the Drenykin have wolf protectors too?" Jack asked.

"They do," replied Angus, who hovered on the perimeter of the crowd. "They look different and smell worse, but you can't expect much else from a hellhound." Giggles rippled through the crowd.

"Hellhound?" Jack interrupted. "So, the Drenykin are evil, like the Devil?"

The young ones laughed. It was good to lighten the mood. Rose smiled. "Some of the Drenykin will seem like the devil when you are faced with them," Rose said, thinking of some of their fiercest warriors. "It's a pity their power is wasted on vengeance."

"A pity?" Rik asked quietly. He looked angry. "You speak as though you don't hate them."

"I knew many of them before the rebellion," Rose answered calmly. "They were not evil then. And just like a powerful Fatum is beauty incarnate, a powerful Drenykin is ... well, at the very least, it's a waste of talent."

The children looked confused but Rose was getting tired. She decided it was time to wrap things up for the night.

"You said the Great Tree protects us. What do you mean?" asked Travis.

"The Great Tree is not only a part of our lifeline to the Earth Mother and necessary for half-human descendants to receive their powers, but it also protects us from human view. Our shield encompasses the Sider lands, waterways, and sky surrounding our commune. When a human looks for us, they see only the forest, the water, and the sky. They can see us in our human forms, but not in our Fatum forms. This is what allows us to be ourselves during our annual reunion. We need not fear being exposed to humans.

"There are exceptions, of course. Michael, for instance, is a human but he was able to see Jack and Travis in their Fatum forms when they came falling out of the sky. The reason for this is because Julea has always been honest with him about our powers. He chose not to believe it until he saw it with his own eyes. But it had not been hidden from him. Once a human knows about our powers, it becomes easier for them to see us in our Fatum forms."

"Does the Great Tree also protect us from the Drenykin?" Jack asked.

"I'm afraid not," Rose replied. "We have guards posted, including Angus' pack, at all times. Encounters with the Drenykin are not uncommon. It was only yesterday that Travis Ryked killed a hellhound on the other side of the river."

A collective gasp went up from the new recruits. Travis shrugged apologetically at Jack. Rose went on.

"Outside the property line, we must not be detected. Our first priority is to pursue The Cause as the Creator has instructed. You will soon see the depths of our operations and you will be amazed. We must also wage war against the Drenykin and equally resist their efforts to convert us to their beliefs."

"But what is the danger in that?" It was Jack. Such a bright boy. Rose began again to feel sad for the war. The wasted youth. She hoped the spark in his eyes would never disappear as it all too often did among warriors.

"I am sure you have many more questions, but I daresay most will be answered by the prophecy itself. It is late now and I think we have all heard enough for one night. Tomorrow night, beside this fire, I will share with our newest warriors the words of the Prophecy recited to us in our dreams that fateful day. Tomorrow, I will give you The Knowledge."

Michael

If he hadn't seen two dragons come crashing out of the sky and turn into Jack and Travis, he would never have believed it. His own son, whom he knew well enough to know that he couldn't fake a dragon, had transformed before his very eyes. But this was insanity. Why would he even consider his son faking a dragon? A flying, fire-breathing, giant black-and-red dragon the size of a house! It terrified the crap out of him.

In Michael's opinion, all things supernatural belonged in the categories of "Not Real" and "Silly Superstition." But Michael could not deny what he had seen with his own eyes.

Julea was calm. "Honey, please say something," she begged quietly. "I know this comes as a shock, but I never hid it from you. You chose not to believe me."

Years and years of Julea's foolish teasing scrolled through his mind.

"Of course, my brother is short, he's an elf."

"Don't mind my mother. She's cranky because she caught her wing on a twig this morning."

"The family reunion is a place where we can be ourselves and practice our powers."

"One day Jack and Abby will be like me and have special powers too."

"It was probably some dust pixies who kept the house clean."

There were too many times to count. Yes, Julea had told him that her family were only half human. But it was so ridiculous that Michael had never really believed her.

Secretly, he suspected she was crazy. It was his parents' opinion that she was certifiable.

Michael loved his wife. He loved her enough to pretend that she was joking when she made occasional references to her family's "powers." He loved her enough to move far away from his disapproving parents. The fact that she had been telling the truth all along hit him all at once like a fire truck to the face.

"Well, I have no choice but to believe you now," Michael spoke angrily. "My son was a dragon today before my very eyes. Now you tell me that my daughter is a mermaid. And my own wife…my own wife…"

"I am the same person I have always been, Michael." Julea was so patient and calm. *How could she be so calm?*

"So, everything your grandmother said at the fire tonight is true? All of the people here are part, uh, Fatum? I am the only person here who doesn't have any powers?"

"There are others. Rik's wife, Charlene. Frank McAllister. I invited you to reunions in the past but you didn't want to come. I'm sorry that you had to learn the truth this way," Julea whispered.

"Yeah. Me too," Michael replied. "It's a lot to take in. I think I'll go out for some fresh air."

"Okay," said Julea. "But don't chain-smoke yourself to death."

"Yeah, I gotta quit this filthy habit one of these days," he said. He avoided Julea's eyes as he headed out the door. Today was not the day to quit smoking.

Jack

After the fire, everyone changed. *Literally.*

The cute, happy girls fluttered around cutely and happily in their tree nymph forms. Grandma Dianna, too, seemed to prefer her pixie form for everything except baking.

It turned out faeries were master decorators. Jack marvelled at their skill when he wasn't distracted by the water sprites, dwarves, and centaurs carousing animatedly in every corner of the property.

He learned that a "Green Tree" was a Fatum child just before he or she got her powers. Until the last Green Tree went through the change, all other Fatum at the reunion kept their human-like forms. But after the first Fire of the Elders, the congregated Fatum wore their supernatural forms with pride.

Uncle Rik was an elf. "It's the whole reason we love the reunion so much," he explained to Jack. "The only other time we use our supernatural forms is during missions. This is our chance each year to be comfortable in our own skin or scales, or whatever the case may be. That is why there is a festive feel to it even though we're here to talk war. Even though my sister is suffering in the hands of the enemy right now." Rik took a deep breath. He stared at the fire. For several moments, he seemed to be somewhere else. Finally, he turned back to Jack as if there'd been no pause. "We all can't help but enjoy this time while it lasts. Of course, you're blessed to live here. You can change form whenever you like."

"So, Aunty Lacey is alive?" asked Jack. He had many questions but not for Uncle Rik. He would ask his mother later. For now, it was this one question that he needed to hear the answer to immediately.

"Yes," replied Rik. "She's alive, whatever that means." He looked Jack in the eye. "I think she's been gone long enough, don't you?"

"Yes," replied Jack. Had she been a hostage for three years? Jack shuddered at the thought.

"Well, don't you worry, Buds," Uncle Rik's voice turned warm and friendly. "We're going to get her out of there. Don't you worry."

Jack nodded lamely. "Uncle Rik. Where's Sam? I want to apologize to her for what happened. I feel terrible."

"It's okay, Jack," Rik assured him. "Sam is resting right now. It took a lot out of her, but she survived. Her powers will be great. She is a blessing to The Cause. It is very rare for a Fatum to be born out of fire and survive. Samantha will be revered among our people and remembered for all of eternity. She will thank you, in time, once she's used to her new form. Have patience with her until then."

"Thanks, Uncle Rik," Jack said. He turned to leave.

"Hey Jack," Rik stopped him.

"Yes?"

"Teej was right. A dragon is a good one. Congratulations and welcome to the 'Faery Corps.'"

"Thanks," Jack mumbled. He tipped his head goodbye and walked away from Rik's small cooking fire. His mind swam with questions about Fatum, Aunt Lacey, and the war. But mostly he thought about flying. He headed toward his tree psyching himself up for a high dive.

Rose

Fatum warriors surrounded the second Fire of the Elders, their faces turned to her. She couldn't look them in the eyes by the time she'd told her story. The young ones. She didn't have to see them. She could feel them. The excitement. The pull. The compulsion that drugged them.

Everyone was like that in the beginning. Before their first battles. But who was she kidding? It was always like that for the warriors. The moment when war fell around them, all misgivings disappeared and exultation took over. Rose reckoned it was the Creator's gift to get them through their service in the Faery Corps. If it was war they were destined to wage, then a gift to embrace it was welcome.

From her perspective, however, there was no exultation. There was no excitement. Only sorrow for the wasted lives. She could almost have been a Drenykin, so disillusioned was she.

Her role as Elder and Matriarch kept her going when hopelessness set in. The war had claimed so many of her children. Her children's children. Some who survived were only shells of their earlier selves.

But how could she have turned Drenykin with her repugnance towards killing? She couldn't have. This must be how the Creator feels, wondering when his children will find peace.

She glanced around briefly before turning in for the night. She had no desire for festivities. That was for the young ones. Let them enjoy it while it lasts.

Across the fire, Abby Sider blushed and smiled at Cash McAllister. The Final Chosen One and Her Protector. For now, it was only words to Abby. Words she didn't understand the meaning of. What those words would mean for Abby … *it was unthinkable.*

Rose sighed as she watched her great-granddaughter chatting animatedly with her peers. In a few days, Abby would be told that she is the Final Chosen One. The One who would save the Earth Mother from humanity's destruction. *Or not.*

"What's wrong, Mom?" Rose turned to find Torrents looking at her worriedly.

"You caught me," she replied. "I fear it will be my time to go soon. But there are so many of you still to take care of. Who will do it when I'm gone?" She chuckled but she meant every word. "Who will take care of you? Or your grand-daughter over there who has the unfortunate fate as the Final Chosen One during the End Times? Who will take care of Kade?"

"Mom, it's like I've said a thousand times, you need to stop worrying about everyone else. If you really plan to die soon, then start spending the life you have left enjoying yourself." Torrents' words were firm but his voice was gentle.

Rose knew she had tears in her eyes but she didn't hide them. She'd never hidden her feelings from any of her children. "I know, Honey. Thank you for reminding me." She scanned the crowd again looking for something joyous. She saw Michael staring across the fire with an angry look on his face. Rose turned to see Abby staring shamelessly into the eyes of Cash McAllister on the brink of a kiss.

"Oh my," Rose whispered. "Will you look at that? The father of the Chosen One wants to protect her from Her Protector." With that, she burst into laughter. This time her tears were caused by joy.

"That's more like it, Mom," Torrents approved.

Teej

Teej was relieved that Dad was keeping Grandma Rose busy. That woman had eyes like a hawk. She could sense a deception faster than anyone. Dad had assured him she was blinded by love when it came to her own family members. But Teej wasn't convinced. He preferred having that loose end covered. They would have to leave tonight before Abby found out her fate. The last thing they needed was one of the Elders catching on to their plan.

It was hard to say goodbye to Kayley. As he had many times in the past, Teej thanked his good fortune for falling in love with another Fatum. The others with human spouses didn't always find comfort and understanding when leaving for battle. Fatum mothers, at least, understood the deep compulsion that beckoned their partners off to war. Kayley would be coming too if it weren't for the boys. Another silent thank you that Kayley was unbidden – a state of grace experienced by Fatum mothers of young children which enabled them to be free from the compulsion to fight.

Teej knew the day would come again when the twins were grown with powers of their own, and Kayley would return to the battlefield to fight by his side. If he lived to see that day, he would have another thing to be thankful for. In the meantime, he liked his beautiful wife spending her days in relative safety; raising their sons to be strong and thoughtful. So, one day they could survive in battle too.

"What are you thinking about," Kayley asked him as she peered into his eyes. They embraced by the large bonfire, enjoying the heat and their last moments together.

"I'm thinking about you and the boys," he told her honestly.

"I'll be here when you get back," she promised. "Then we'll go home to the boys. Just don't let Rik do anything foolish and get you killed."

"He's not like that in battle. You remember," Teej gently admonished her. Rik was a loose cannon in some respects. But there wasn't anyone he'd rather have beside him in battle. His instincts were impeccable.

Kayley sighed. "Yes, I remember. It's just that I don't see that side of him much anymore."

"I know, Toots," Teej soothed. "I know. Don't worry. I'm a tough son-of-a-gun, myself."

"I know," she replied sincerely.

They didn't speak after that. They held each other tight until Rik gave the signal that it was time to go.

Abby

The last thing her mother said to her was: "Stay close to your uncles." What did that mean?

Abby watched the house disappear from view as they rounded a corner. She didn't want to leave in the first place but her mother insisted. "Uncle Rik and Uncle Teej need you," she'd said.

"Listen to your mother," Uncle Rik instructed. "You gotta show us where the new store is."

It was a one street town. How hard could it be?

"Oh, come on," teased Uncle Teej. "Go for a drive with your uncles. We hardly ever see you." So, Abby agreed. She told Cash to meet her by the fire. She'd be back in two hours. Abby sighed. Two hours she'd never get back. Two hours she could have spent with Cash.

Abby wasn't sure if Michael had put two and two together about the McAllister wolves, but she knew it wouldn't be long before he would. He would know about her deception all those months. She shivered at the thought.

Uncle Rik was unusually quiet. His face was drawn, like he had a lot on his mind. As he maneuvered around the potholes on the dirt road, he seemed to be gritting his teeth. Uncle Teej was his usual light-hearted self, but there was an edge to his humour tonight. He sat sideways so he could talk to Abby in the back seat.

"How are you feeling tonight, Abby?" he asked. "Was The Knowledge what you expected? Are you revved up to serve in the corps? Or do you want to get trained first?"

He was referring to the "school" that Lyll was attending for new recruits.

"Well, I've never really liked school," she replied. "I think I'd rather learn in the field."

Rik spoke then. "It isn't that kind of school. I didn't like school either when I was a kid. But this school is way better. You should do both. Start in the field but go back and get your training later."

That seemed silly to Abby, but she didn't want to be rude. If she was going to get the training, she would do it first. "Yeah, maybe," she answered noncommittally.

They drove on in silence. When they neared the end of the dirt road bordering Beaverdell, Rik spoke again.

"It's like this, Abby; we'd like you to begin your service right now. You can get some training from Teej and I as we go. But mostly you will need to depend on yourself. We are going to the frontlines. This is called guerrilla warfare. The three of us are going up against about thirty or more Drenykin and hounds. We are going in to get Lacey." He paused momentarily. "We brought you out here to ask you if you'll join us."

Abby was stunned. *What? Huh? We're not going to the store?* The questions formed in her mind but not on her lips.

"Give her a moment, Bro," Teej said.

"I don't understand." Abby stammered. The whole conversation seemed surreal.

"We're going to get your Aunt," replied Rik, "It's dangerous but you will have your uncles. We need your help, Abby. Will you join us?"

Teej explained. "You can go back home now, Abby. We won't force you to come with us. But we need someone with your powers to help us. The Elders don't know that we're doing this, so we have to be discreet. We trust you not to say anything if you do go back now."

"But won't we get in trouble?" asked Abby. "Mom will freak …"

"Your mother knows," Rik interrupted. "She and Duke are the only other people who know."

"And Grandpa Torrents," Teej added.

"He doesn't know we brought Abby," Rik answered.

"You mean now?" Abby asked. "You're leaving right now?" Cash was waiting for her by the fire. How could she leave and not return? She couldn't even tell him with her mind because the telepathy only worked when they were near each other.

"Yes," replied Rik. "We're leaving right now. Lacey has been in the hands of those savages for long enough." He practically growled when he spoke. "If you decide not to join us, you'll have to swim home because Teej and I aren't going back."

Abby couldn't decide. The more she thought about going with her uncles, the more excited she became. It was like an invisible force pulled her towards her Aunt Lacey, wherever she was. But she felt an equal pull back to Cash. It was a connection that she'd experienced ever since she'd met him. It felt wrong to leave him.

Sensing her Uncle Rik's impatience, she spoke. "Why me?"

"We need someone with your powers that we can trust," Rik replied.

"We trust you, Abby," added Teej. "We are disobeying the Elders to do this. They're taking their sweet time getting Lacey out of there. We aren't willing to wait any longer."

"But what are they waiting for?" Abby asked. She agreed that almost three years of captivity was more than enough. And she knew firsthand that it had been almost ten months since Lacey had been located.

"I don't know what they're waiting for, but I know why they're not in a hurry," Rik replied angrily. "It is because Lacey is a unicorn like your mother."

Abby was confused. "What does that have to do with it?"

"Unicorns are very special for many reasons," Teej explained. "In particular, anyone who kills a unicorn is cursed for life. The Elders know that no Drenykin would ever kill a unicorn for fear of the curse."

"We can brief you on everything you need to know if you come with us," Rik said. "But I am impatient to get going. Are you with us or not?"

Silence filled the air inside the little car. Abby looked from one to the other of her uncle's expectant faces. How could she say no? Her mother had sent her. In her heart, there was only one answer.

"Yes. I'm with you."

PART FOUR

THE CAUSE
AND THE
CASUALTIES

Let it be known that Descendants of the Tree
shall be Protectors of The Mother and
Descendants of the Wolf shall be Protectors of the Tree.
Your tribes shall sacrifice your lives for The Cause.

Travis

For the first time in his life, everything made sense. Travis went through phases of grief, anger, remorse, fear, relief, and resolve. His mother had not abandoned him after all. While Jack practiced his powers in the night sky, Travis sat at Julea's kitchen table.

"That day in the grocery store, your mother didn't forget you there," Julea explained gently after the second Fire of the Elders. "We believe she was kidnapped by a Drenykin captain named Jerematicus." Travis' body vibrated with the need to go out and kill.

"You know that feeling you got when you received The Knowledge, that overwhelming loyalty to The Cause and compulsion to right the wrongs? When a Fatum mother gets pregnant, that feeling is replaced with a compulsion to protect her Fatum offspring which lasts until all of her children have received their powers. Your mother didn't call out for you when she was taken because she didn't want them to get you too."

They spoke for an hour or so. Travis was relieved that his mother was alive. He felt an urge that was painful to kill all the sorry suckers who dared to hurt or control her. He felt sick with the need to find her. He didn't know how he would do it, but Travis would find out where his mother was. Then he would bring her home. He couldn't help himself. He had no choice.

After their chat, Travis needed to blow off some steam. Or maybe just breathe a little fire. He smiled to himself and set off in search of Jack. Although Jack was black against the black of night, you couldn't miss his flames burning up the sky every few moments. Travis wondered how he could get close enough to absorb Jack's powers.

As he was looking up at the sky, pondering his dilemma, he walked right smack into his cousin Samantha.

"Whoa, what are you doing?" Travis asked, irritated and embarrassed that he'd been caught unaware like that.

"I'm sorry," Samantha replied. "I think I'm blending in with my environment again." She blushed deeply, then turned serious. "I was actually coming to find you."

Before she could explain, they heard a loud screech overhead and were blasted by a huge gust of wind. Looking up, Travis watched as Jack lowered himself out of the sky, his wings batting the air in an effort to descend slowly and carefully. Each bat of his wings sent another gust of wind down onto them. Jack trampled two trees and sat hard on a third as his feet and body met the ground. His tail swished involuntarily colliding with a fourth. Apples rained to the ground in a deluge.

Travis was floored by the vast size of his friend. He watched as the massive dragon suddenly disappeared leaving a diminutive teenage boy sitting in the center of the devastation.

"Geez," said Jack. "I gotta work on that." He looked at the trees he'd broken and shook his head. "I'm so sorry," he said to them.

"They'll be okay. Jack, Travis, I need to talk to you guys," Samantha said impatiently.

"That was incredible!" Jack said excitedly. "I'm a dragon!"

"Yeah, we know," Travis replied tolerantly. "I was planning to join you but I couldn't figure out how to get up there. It turns out I can only make the change when I'm within about 25 feet of the one whose powers I'm absorbing."

"So, you can change right now?" Jack asked, grinning. "Let's go back up." He rubbed his hands together eagerly. Travis began to feel the newly familiar tingly sensation spreading all over him.

"WAIT!" Samantha exclaimed, stopping them both from making the change. "I need to talk to you guys." She turned to Travis. "It's about your mom. I know where she is."

Travis would have stopped it if he could, but years of built-up pain and rage bloomed out of him. Before he knew it, he was on all fours with the upper body of a boy and the lower body of a salamander.

Julea

"When will your brothers be back with Abby?" Michael asked when they laid together in bed later that night. Family members still crowded around the large fire, but Michael liked all the kids to be in bed before he went to sleep. Julea had known this moment would come.

"I've never lied to you," she whispered. "I've had no choice. Unicorn's can hold back the truth. But we can never lie." She hesitated before finishing. "Abby's not coming back tonight."

"What?" replied Michael, confused. He sat up and faced her. "What are you talking about? I thought they were going to the store. Where could they possibly be going overnight with Abby?"

Julea was silent. The words came to her in different variations but none of them made it to her lips. *How do I say this?*

"Okay, how about this question," Michael said, becoming more agitated with Julea's silence. "When *will* Abby be home?"

"I don't know," replied Julea honestly. The truth devastated her. What if she didn't come back? Her faith in the Creator was the only thing keeping her sane at the moment. The Creator would not let the Final Chosen One die before she's even begun. Julea steeled herself. She forced the words out without feeling them. It was the only way. "Abby has gone with my brothers to bring back my sister."

Michael seemed shocked. "Lacey? Your sister, Lacey?"

"Yes," she replied. "My sister. They've gone to get my sister."

"But I thought she was dead," Michael said exasperatedly. "I thought we inherited her house!"

"We never knew for sure she was dead, Michael. I told you she wasn't dead. I never believed she was dead. She's not dead. She's alive." Julea didn't mention her suspicions. That Lacey was barely alive. That she was kept within an inch of her life. "Her funeral was a cover for an impromptu family meeting. The meeting that decided who would live in this house."

Michael only heard the first part. "Is your sister coming from the airport? Are they going to pick her up?" It would have been a good cover if she could lie.

"Michael, listen to me. Abby went with my brothers to rescue my sister. They need her because… because…"

"Why Julea? Why do they need Abby? What is going on here?" Michael must have sensed that something was wrong. He was getting very upset. Julea could not reassure him. Something *was* very wrong. Their daughter was risking her life. No. The fact was, Julea was risking her daughter's life. Was she choosing her sister over her daughter? Julea wasn't sure she'd made the right decision. How could she have allowed her to go? She burst into tears.

"What Julea? Tell me what is going on here?" Michael demanded again. "Damnit Julea, tell me WHAT is going on?"

A sudden calm came over Julea. Her emotional armour had arrived. "Okay," she said. All traces of tears were gone. "I know you're not going to like this, but here is the truth. They took Abby with them because she is the Final Chosen One and they needed insurance that the Elders would order backup if they run into trouble…"

Julea told the whole story as Michael stared at her in disbelief and horror. It took her breath away. She saw accusation in his eyes. She saw herself in his eyes.

Samantha

"Whoa, Man!" Jack stared at Travis. "What happened to you?"

Travis' lower body was covered in spotted scales. He had short little legs and a long, thick tail. Travis resettled himself upright in the standing position.

Samantha blushed indignantly. "He is an empath so he turned into a salamander. Like me."

"Is that what you look like?" Jack gushed. "Cool!"

"Not exactly," replied Samantha. "I'm much prettier."

Travis looked down at himself. "What can a Salamander do?" he asked.

"We can withstand fire, produce poison in our skin, blend in with our environment, grow new limbs, and our teeth are pretty deadly too," Samantha smiled broadly showing her pointed teeth.

"Cool!" Travis and Jack said together.

Samantha was satisfied with their mutual admiration. She felt a little better about her new powers. But she still wondered what might have been.

Travis had recovered his wits. "Did you say you know where my mother is?" he asked. His tail twitched.

Samantha looked intensely from one boy to the other, deciding how to start.

"Last year, my dad went out to the store and didn't return for several months," she began. "Mother spent hours on the phone with him … talking him down."

"What do you mean, 'talking him down?'" asked Jack.

"I'm not sure. I could hear him yelling angrily into the phone, but I couldn't make out the words. Mom held the phone to her ear tightly and walked away.

"One day he called and I answered the phone. I asked him point blank where he was and why he hadn't come home. He told me he was spying on the people who stole his sister. He told me he was waiting for his chance to get her out."

"Well, why didn't he get her out then?" Travis asked angrily.

"He said the house was heavily guarded. He would get himself and Lacey both killed if he tried. For the first time in my life, my father cried to me. He was distraught."

She paused remembering. She had felt so helpless.

"So, what's your point?" asked Travis. "Your dad told you where my mom is?"

"Not exactly," admitted Samantha. "My dad and I came here right before the reunion. He had a private meeting with Uncle Teej and Aunty Julea at the fort. That's when they made a plan to rescue Aunty Lacey."

"But if it was a private meeting, then how do you know about it? Did your dad tell you?" Jack asked.

Samantha looked at their faces wondering if they could see her guilt. "I followed my dad and hid under the window," she admitted. "I was almost caught when Bosco found me in the shadows. But he must have recognized me, because he just licked me and ran off."

Jack chuckled. "Dumb dog."

"So, you found out where my mom is that night?" Travis asked.

"I'll make this as short and sweet as I can," replied Samantha. "Basically, my dad left with Uncle Teej and Abby tonight to go save your mom. But before he left, he tattooed a map on Grandpa Torrents' back. I believe that map will tell us where your mom is."

It must have been too much information at once. The boys spoke together.

"Abby went where?" Jack demanded.

"A map tattoo?" Travis questioned skeptically.

Samantha ignored Jack. "My dad always leaves a map or two behind to let people know where to find him in an emergency. I've looked everywhere, but I haven't been able to find any maps this time. Last night, I stopped by the fort to see if Lyll wanted to come out. My dad was there. Grandpa Torrents was under the needle. Uncle Duke was there and all three of them were talking real quiet. As soon as I saw the tattoo, I knew my dad would be leaving soon."

"So, you're saying he left tonight?" Jack asked. "And that he took Abby?"

"I'm saying, they've gone to save Aunty Lacey. I'm saying your sister is the Final Chosen One."

Cash

He waited two hours by the fire. Then another hour. A little after eleven o'clock, Michael appeared next to him smoking a cigarette. Cash was immediately uncomfortable. Was he going to get mad about Cash coming onto the property in his wolf form all these months?

Michael looked into the fire while he spoke. "She's not coming back tonight," he said. Cash was caught off guard.

"Who's not coming back?" he asked.

Michael faced him and looked him in the eyes. "Abby." For a moment Michael looked almost as if he felt sorry for Cash. Then he turned his back and walked away.

Cash's heart began to pound. His ears rang as the words penetrated. Abby wasn't coming back tonight. Well, where was she going then? His skin began to prickle as his well-formed instincts jumped to sudden conclusions. *Abby is in danger,* they said. *You must find her,* his instincts screamed.

Jack

"I'm not doing it. You do it," said Jack.

"Why can't Sam do it?" Travis replied.

"I'm a girl!" Samantha exclaimed. "I can't go down there and take a picture of Grandpa Torrents' naked butt!" She giggled and blushed.

"He'll put his pants on if you go," Jack assured her. "He does for Abby. He says a man has to have a little consideration for the ladies. Says he leaves his pants off for the men so they know who's boss." Travis laughed.

"Lalalalala," Samantha sang with her fingers in her ears. "I can't hear you."

"Sorry," Jack said. "I guess I still need to learn a little consideration for the ladies." He mimicked Grandpa Torrents' voice.

"It's okay," said Samantha. "But if we're going to be travelling together, maybe you can work on it."

"Okay," Jack promised. "So, here is my camera. Just tell him you want a picture for your dad's portfolio."

"Good idea," Samantha said. "I wonder if he'll let me."

"He will," replied Jack. "He's a sucker for his grandchildren." They all nodded and laughed. Jack could not think of a time in his life when Grandpa Torrents had said no to him. This was going to be easy.

"We'll meet back at the new clearing with our packs at dusk. Dress warm, Sam," Jack said seriously.

"Oh, don't worry," said Samantha. "I will."

Torrents

He put his clothes on when Samantha arrived. He didn't want to make her feel uncomfortable. The day his grandchildren felt uncomfortable around him was a day Torrents Ryked vowed he would never see. Family was everything. Nothing else mattered.

"Hey there, my little darlin'," he greeted her. "Want some coffee or tea?"

"Uh, maybe some tea would be good," Samantha answered hesitantly. Torrents could tell she had something on her mind.

"Alright, I'll just put this kettle over the fire then, Sweetie." He busied himself giving her a chance to figure out what she wanted to say. Torrents suspected it had something to do with her father.

"Um, Grandpa Torrents," Samantha began. "I was wondering if I could take a picture of your newest tattoo for my dad's portfolio. I, uh, forgot to ask you yesterday.

It's my job. I keep Dad's portfolio up to date. Um, I volunteered to do it."

Torrents was no fool. He answered quickly. "Sure, Angel. Of course, you can." He wondered why she wanted the map. Was she planning to follow her dad?

He took his time getting her tea ready. ZZ-Top blared from an old cd player. He thought of many ways to ask the question but in the end, it came out very direct.

"So, you're planning to follow your dad, then?"

Samantha looked stunned. The colour had drained from her face. "Umm," she said. Torrents watched her eyes and waited. This mission was much too dangerous for a new recruit. If she had any intention of interfering, he would have to stop her.

Her face betrayed her emotions one by one. Shock, fear, indecision, resignation, determination. He wasn't sure if she was determined to tell the truth or lie.

"You're right. I want to follow my dad."

Torrents already had great esteem for his grand-daughter but her honesty made him admire her even more. He regretted that he had to put his foot down.

"Well, I'm sorry to hear that because unfortunately I can't let you do that."

"Why not?" Samantha asked defiantly. "I was born out of fire. I'm practically invincible."

"Well, that's true, Angel. But you're also young and inexperienced."

"What do you mean? I'm the same age as Abby!"

"What does that have to do with it?" Torrents asked mildly. He didn't want to upset her.

"They took Abby with them," Samantha replied. "Why couldn't they take me with them too?"

In the back of his mind, Torrents took note of Samantha's bruised ego. But it was the new information that jarred him. They took Abby. He was in disbelief. Samantha must be mistaken.

"Why do you think they took Abby?" he asked carefully.

"I watched them leave. They pretended they were going to the store, but I knew Dad was leaving. I can tell when he's starting a mission. He gets more and more high-strung as the departure date approaches. And he starts leaving maps in strange places," Samantha said, smiling ironically.

"Well, little darlin', if what you're saying is true, and they took Abby with them, then we have a problem."

"Why is that a problem?" Samantha asked. "Didn't you know she was going?"

"No, I didn't. And if I did, I would have stopped them. It's a problem because this is an extremely dangerous mission and Abby is the Final Chosen One. Your father shouldn't be risking her life for anything."

"Maybe that's why they took her." Samantha's first instinct was to defend her dad. "Maybe Abby is the only one who can save Lacey."

At the sound of her name, Torrents winced with pain. His heart had felt raw and torn since she'd first gone missing. Every slight remembrance of the situation brought fresh waves of nausea and heartache.

"Abby's fate does not lie in saving Lacey," he told Samantha sadly. "The Cause is much bigger than one Fatum. We have always known this. Are you done your tea? Because I think you and I need to go and have a talk with my eldest daughter. I cannot believe she agreed to this crazy plan."

"What crazy plan?" Samantha asked. Torrents felt sorry for her. Was this the end of her innocence?

"If they took Abby with them, there can only be one reason," he replied. He stood up, pulled his hair into a ponytail, then turned towards the path. "Let's go my little angel. I want to hear what Julea's got to say about it."

A half hour later, Julea was in a puddle of tears. Her confession was quick and concise. "Yes, Abby went with them. Yes, I let her go." Every word after came out like a purge between sniffs and sobs. "I think I made the wrong decision. But we have to save Lacey. But Abby's just a little girl. But Teej says they'll protect her. Oh Dad! Can you please go and get her!"

"You're not coming?" Torrents was surprised. He knew Julea to be fearless in battle.

She pulled him aside where Samantha wouldn't hear her. Fresh tears slid down her cheeks as she whispered, "We haven't told the kids yet, but I'm pregnant."

Torrents comforted his daughter as best he could. He promised to go get Abby. He really had no choice at this point. He was the only one with a map.

Jack

The "new clearing" was the flattened area where Jack had made his ungracious descent earlier that day. When they met there that night, there were four extra guests. Grandpa Torrents, who rather than try to stop them had fortunately decided to join them with his map. Cash, who had been sneaking around in the trees listening to them make their plans and now demanded to accompany them. And most surprisingly, Jack's parents, Julea and Michael.

Mom came to give her blessing and a few gems of advice. Jack felt somewhat betrayed that she wasn't trying to stop him. Wasn't she worried for his safety? She seemed to read his mind.

"Can I convince you to stay?" she whispered as she embraced him. He looked into her eyes. The pain and fear he saw shamed him. Of course, she was worried.

"No," he replied. "But I promise to try and come back."

His mother smiled through thick tears. "Stay close to Grandpa Torrents," she said quietly. She held his face in her hands and looked into his eyes. "Rest often. Don't eat bad food no matter how hungry you are. And kill them before they kill you."

That was a first. Permission to commit murder. Jack nodded his head lamely as he was pulled in for another hug.

"Oh, and don't worry about these trees," she added, gesturing to the trampled remains of Jack's earlier attempt at landing. "I will treat them. They will be okay."

"I love you, Mom," replied Jack.

"I love you too. Fly safe and take good care of your father."

Jack was confused. His father?

"I'm coming with you, Jack," Dad said. Jack turned to face him. "To get Abby."

"Um, okay," Jack replied.

"I'm going too," Cash informed Jack's mother. Cash looked pale. He had a wild look in his eyes. It reminded Jack of his cousin, a drug addict.

"I'm glad you are," Julea answered knowingly. She crossed the small space and folded Cash into a hug.

"Okay, well that settles it," Grandpa Torrents announced. "Samantha's coming with me. Jack, you phase first. Your dad is riding with you. Travis next. You're taking Cash."

Jack nodded to his mother ignoring the stab through his heart when he saw her tears. He phased into a dragon and knelt to let Michael climb on. Then he lifted off into the sky, hovering above the clearing while Travis made the change. They had practiced together all day. Cash climbed onto Travis' back. They rose gently into the air beside Jack.

Grandpa Torrents was the last to make the change. Although he was much smaller than Jack and Travis in their dragon forms, he was a majestic, muscular creature with a commanding presence. He had the feathered upper body of a bald eagle, with wings, and front claws. The rear half of his body was covered in fur, with the legs and tail of a lion.

So, that's what a griffin looks like, thought Jack.

Samantha looped a strong rope around Grandpa Torrents' neck, then threw her leg over his back. He flapped his powerful wings, rising into the sky effortlessly. He squawked twice, a high-pitched melody, before heading over the trees, away from the Sider lands.

There was only one thing for Jack and Travis to do. Follow him.

Abby

A scream awoke her. Her scream. She lay there, panting and sweating, in the dark hotel room.

"What's wrong," asked Uncle Rik, coming into her room. He lit a candle beside her bed and stared into her eyes. "Bad dream?"

"No," said Abby irrationally. "It was real."

Uncle Teej appeared in the doorway. "Is everything alright?" he asked.

"She was dreaming," Rik answered. "It was just a bad dream."

"No," Abby repeated. "It was real." She sat in the bed shaking, trying to understand what she was telling her uncles. She wasn't sure how it was possible, but she knew she had been there.

"I have nightmares all the time, Abby," Rik soothed her. "They seem very real at the time, but once you're more awake you'll realize it was just a dream. Everything is okay."

"What were you dreaming about?" Teej asked. "Sometimes talking about it helps."

"The matchstick man," Abby replied. "I was tied to a chair with IVs in my arms. He was taking my blood. I can still smell him. I can still smell the blood." Abby shuddered, trying not to gag. Only moments ago, she'd felt her life force being drained out of her.

Uncle Rik jumped at her words. "What did you say?" he asked. Teej came into the room.

"I couldn't see very well. His hair was white. He was laughing at me. He held a wooden unicorn."

Rik and Teej looked at each other. "Jerematicus," they said at the same time.

"Yes!" Abby replied. "That was what they called him. How did you know?"

"Listen to me, Abby," Rik replied. "You are right. You weren't dreaming. It was a vision. My sister sent you a vision."

"What do you mean?" Abby asked.

"She's showing you what she sees so you can help us find her," Teej explained.

Rik was excited. "Lacey is communicating with us through you, Abby," he said. "You have to try to remember every detail. Tell us what you saw."

Abby shuddered. The images were distinct but painful. She couldn't believe her aunt had been surviving like this, bound to a chair being slowly bled to death. How could anyone endure such horror?

"Abby, listen to me," Teej spoke gently. "We need you to think back to your vision. Who was in the room with you other than Jerematicus? What did the room look like? How is Lacey holding up? How bad is it?"

Abby stared into her uncles' expectant faces. "There was only me, Jerematicus, and another man. I didn't see what he looked like. And one woman. She was behind me. She never spoke, but I felt her presence. It felt like she was kind."

"That was your aunt," Rik told her. "Visions are always like that. The person sending the vision is there too."

Abby hoped she wouldn't have to go through it again. "Why me?" she asked timidly, ashamed that she couldn't handle briefly what her aunt was surviving continuously.

"Only Lacey can answer that," Rik replied. "Now tell us everything you know. It's time to rock and roll, ladies and gentlemen. We'll spend the day strategizing. Then tonight, we go in."

Michael

They holed up in a small house in Downtown Kelowna on the wrong side of the lake, as far as Michael was concerned. The owner of the house was a small-boned Fatum woman named Figgy who made cement gargoyles for a living. She went about her business quietly in the kitchen while they congregated in the attached dining room.

Cash stalked the front yard in his wolf form. As soon as they had landed, he'd changed. His fur stood on end. He growled viciously in frustration at anyone who got close.

"No one is going to believe that's a dog in the front yard," Michael worried aloud.

Figgy laughed. "Don't you worry about him," she advised. "My neighbours are used to seeing strange animals around here. They learned a long time ago not to make a fuss about it." She chuckled again without explaining.

Michael turned back to Torrents. "Tell me again what we're doing here? And why can't we use two-way radios?"

"We can't just storm in there," explained his father-in-law in his gruffy voice. "It might disrupt whatever Rik's already got in place. We'd be risking their lives. And two-way radios are easily discovered by Drenykin. They would announce our arrival before we even arrive."

"We're risking Abby's life by letting her go in without us," Michael insisted. "I don't care what your Fatum way of doing things is," Michael sneered. "My daughter needs me with her right now."

Torrents' face grew grim. Michael wondered if he'd gone too far. He'd heard of Torrents' anger, but he'd never seen it firsthand. But Torrents was deadly calm. "What do you suggest?" he said bitingly.

"I'm sorry, Torrents," Michael placated. "It's just hard to sit here knowing Abby could…get hurt. I feel like I need to be doing something. Can't you just create a distraction of some sort on the property, while I zip in and get her?"

"Well, for one thing, we don't know if she's there. For another, I don't think you've considered the other lives that are at stake." Torrents replied. "You are not the only one with children, Michael."

"Yeah, what about my mom!" Travis burst out indignantly.

Michael's cheeks flamed. He'd barely gotten used to the idea of Fatum, never mind war. A part of him was tempted to bail on his wife's family. This wasn't the peaceful life he'd always planned. Even so, he knew he'd do the right thing.

"Okay, so we don't know where Rik, Teej, and Abby are. But we know Lacey is in the house. So, this is obviously where we start with our plan," Michael said. Someone had to take charge. Torrents seemed capable but Michael didn't trust anyone right now. Not after his own wife had thrown their daughter to the wolves.

Torrents turned his back so they could examine the tattooed map for the umpteenth time.

"We know that there is no road into the property, so there are only three ways in. Walking, flying, or by boat. We know that the property is inhabited by wolves."

"Not wolves," said Travis. "Nothing like wolves," he snapped.

"Okay, what am I supposed to call them?" Michael asked mildly. He could only imagine what the boy was going through.

"Massive, stinking, filthy dogs with fangs," Travis replied.

"They smell horrible and they taste worse," Torrents agreed. "They are the real thing. Drenykin, bloody hellhounds."

"It sounds like walking in is risky business," Michael said. "So, we fly in."

It's not as easy as that," replied Torrents. "We cannot fly in undetected. At least on foot, we could attempt to surprise them." He sounded doubtful.

"Well, how do you think Rik and Teej are going in with Abby?" Michael asked.

"I can't be sure," Torrents admitted. "But if it were me, I'd sneak in for the surprise attack. But that's a whole lot easier with three than it is with six, including a dragon."

"So, we split up," Jack suggested logically. "Some of us play the distraction game. The others sneak in and rescue the girls."

"The girls don't need you to rescue them," Samantha said petulantly.

Torrents chuckled. "Don't worry, little darlin'," he assured her. "These young bloods ain't seen nothing yet. Female Fatum are fierce. The Chosen One is always female."

Michael shook his head. There was that phrase again. 'the Chosen One.'

"Torrents, before we go on, I have to ask you one question," Michael said gravely. He looked his father-in-law in the eyes. "Tell me, why is Abby the Chosen One?"

Torrents didn't even pause to think it through. He placed his hand on Michael's shoulder and spoke sincerely. "It is the will of the Creator, Brother. That's all we know."

Dianna

"She hasn't left her bed, Thom. What should we do?" It was Dianna's instinct to do something … anything to help her daughter.

"Let her lie," he replied. "She deserves the rest. We need to think about the baby."

"I am thinking about the baby," Dianna asserted. "She might lose the baby if she doesn't get a hold of herself."

"Her whole family are risking their lives while she stays behind," Thom reasoned. "This is how she's dealing with it, Sweets."

"Lying around in bed won't help anything," Dianna argued. "She's got to keep living. What if one or all of them don't come back?"

Thom nodded. "You're right, Honey. But why don't you let me handle it?" He smiled teasingly. "Julea won't react to me the way she reacts to you."

Dianna thought he might be right. "Okay," she agreed. "Can you do it right now? I've got a bad feeling and I don't know why. But I know we've got to get Julea back on her feet immediately."

Jack

Jack's heart swelled with pride as he watched his father outline his plan. He was the only one without powers in their group, yet he had just as much to offer, if not more. Jack had never pegged his dad to be a master strategist. Grandpa Torrents looked equally impressed.

"Did you just come up with this while flying here last night?" Torrents asked. "Or do you have military background that I'm unaware of?"

"I watch the Knowledge Network," Michael quipped. Jack wondered if that was really where he learned it.

His father turned to him. "Jack, do you understand what we're doing then?"

Jack nodded. "Gramps will fly me up to a cave in the cliff above the property. I'll wait there until Grandpa Torrents sends the signal. If he signals to engage, I'll torch some Drenykin devils to dust. If he signals to withdraw, then I meet you back here."

Jack wasn't sure what he wanted more; a chance to test his powers or a chance to escape without risking his life. He listened as the others repeated their positions and goals.

"I'll disguise myself as a Drenykin hound and distract the others while Cash sneaks in and finds Abby," Travis said.

"If she's on land, I will find her quickly," Cash asserted. He looked at Michael. "But if she's in the water…"

"That's my position," Michael assured him. "If she's in the water, I'll get her." Figgy's boat was tied to a pay dock at the beach. Michael would sail it alone with Samantha swimming alongside him in the water.

"Okay, then," Grandpa Torrents finished. "I will locate my sons and hopefully my daughter. Best-case scenario, we're there to ensure they escape with Lacey. Worst case scenario, we battle. Just remember the goals. Get Lacey and Abby out alive and return before the Elders know we're gone. Let's do this."

Julea

As she lay against the soft ground in her herb garden absorbing the heat of the sun, Julea forced herself to breathe long and deep. For the baby. Stress was not good for the baby. If only they'd return. Then Julea would be able to breathe without thinking about it.

She felt a small flutter of movement on her lower right side. "Hello baby," Julea whispered. She rubbed her belly in the place where she'd felt her child move. Breathing deeply again, Julea pulled herself to sitting.

I guess I should go back soon or Mom will start to worry, she reminded herself. Her stepfather, Thom, had put it gently. "Your mama and I are worried about you," he'd said. "You have to pull yourself together, Julea. This is how it is. They may or may not survive. But you need to survive regardless. If only for the little babe."

Julea knew they were right. But it didn't matter. Getting up and moving around didn't change anything. She walked slowly towards the clearing where she'd last seen her husband and son. All she could do was go through the motions of living, while her heart was in another place with her family.

Abby

Uncle Rik's plan seemed flawless. But Teej warned her nothing ever went according to plan. You've got to be ready for anything, he said. She repeated it in her mind like a mantra hoping it would give her the focus and courage she needed.

She floated invisibly near the surface of the lake with a clear view of the house, waiting for her cue. The waters were strangely quiet. Abby had expected Drenykin water sprites and other warriors guarding the house like Cookies and her squad guarded the Sider property. She was surprised to learn that the lake that lapped against this shore was feared by the Drenykin.

"Many powerful Drenykin have entered that lake never to be seen again," Rik explained to her. "Others have returned raving about a great beast with a long body and a big head and sharp teeth. The beast is resistant to magic and its scales are impenetrable. The Drenykin have learned to stay in their boats."

"But won't the beast come after me?" Abby asked.

"I don't think so," Rik replied. "No Fatum has even been lost in this lake before. I believe the beast is a friend of the Fatum. Folklore tells of times in the past when local humans were rescued from the lake by the beast."

"So, I have nothing to fear?" Abby pushed.

"Your main concern will be to guard the shore from Drenykin arriving by boat. It is unlikely to happen, but possible. If you see a boat approaching, sink it."

"What do you mean, sink it?" Abby asked.

"You know what I mean," Rik had replied. "Raise up that beautiful voice and take the enemy down. Prevent them from interrupting our mission."

"Okay," Abby whispered. But a piece of her wondered if it would really even work. It seemed incredible. Then all of this seemed incredible. Yet it was deathly real.

Now, Abby looked up into the night sky at the dark line of trees surrounding the property. She couldn't see Uncle Teej but she knew he was there somewhere. She shivered in anticipation, despite the warm temperature of the water. The thought shamed her. While she enjoyed the warm, safe water, her aunt was at death's door inside that house. The visions were coming frequently now while she was awake. Brief memories and snapshots from Aunt Lacey's present intruded into Abby's consciousness. She was grateful they came in short bursts. She wouldn't be able to handle it any other way.

By repeatedly sharing the visions that plagued her throughout the day, Abby was able to inform her uncles where her Aunt was held hostage in the house. Rik also had a good idea of how many Drenykin were in the house. The mystery of how Aunt Lacey had arrived was discovered as well. She'd arrived by boat.

Rik's job was to sneak into the house, dispose of Lacey's guards quietly, and get Lacey out of the house. Uncle Teej would break cover, swoop in for Lacey and carry her off the property. Even if the Drenykin warriors didn't see Rik bring her out, they would see Teej fly in. When Abby began to hear their shouts, she was instructed to quickly swim across the lake and meet Teej and Lacey back at Figgy's car.

Abby's heart began to race as that now-familiar feeling came on. Visions from Aunt Lacey assaulted her, flashing through her mind convulsively and painfully ... *Lying below decks, drifting on merciless waves with her mouth gagged and her hands tied. Bound and spat on as she was led onto land. Staring into the laughing faces of Drenykin warriors as she was shoved and kicked through the house. The room she inhabited now. Stark, lonely, and intimidating with its bare walls and putrid stench. The sweet smell of her own blood making her mouth even drier.*

Abby had to remind herself, as she came out of these horrifying visions, that it wasn't the smell of her own blood that still filled her nostrils. It was her aunt's blood. A woman who'd been tortured for the past three years.

It was time to take her home, Abby realized. Aunt Lacey needed to come home. Or Abby might die there with her.

Rik

Lacey sure had some cojones. It was one thing for Rik to bring Abby on the mission and a whole other for Lacey to join their fates. He saw no reason to tell Abby the extent of Lacey's interference. It might scare her. Fear was the last thing a warrior needed going into battle. Anger. Vengeance. Obsession. These things one could work with. Resolve was the best.

He crept among the trees silently. He'd seen at least a dozen hounds so far. None of them had seen him, however. So, he continued. He itched to shed their blood but the mission's success preceded his lust for revenge. Get Lacey out. Send Abby home. Wreak fury on the enemy. In that order.

It was almost too easy for him to approach the house unnoticed. Rik wondered briefly if they were letting him in. But no. He hadn't made a sound. They didn't know he was there.

A few more steps and the house stood before him. It was a large sprawling rancher built from logs, cabin-style, in a rustic but elegant fashion. From Abby's visions, Rik deduced that the bedrooms were at the back of the house. He scanned the windows to get an idea of the layout inside the house.

As he crouched in the shadows of the forest assessing the perimeter, Rik's tattoos glowed like battle marks in the lamplight from the porch. He stretched his neck and flexed his arms, then whistled high and charged like a mockingbird. A few mockingbirds in the vicinity answered sociably.

Rik didn't pause to wonder if Teej and Abby got his cue. He crawled low through the long grass and weeds. He stopped when he was close enough to see how many hounds guarded the door. Rik chuckled silently at the lap dogs before him. Fat and spoiled, he observed humourlessly. Five of them.

Rik wasn't worried about the hounds anyway. His elf powers made him impervious to spells. No alarms would go off alerting the hounds to his presence. He also had the special ability of finding secret doors and hidden passageways. If things went according to plan, he'd be in the house before anyone was the wiser.

He located a trap door and whistled once more to cover the sound of opening it. Then he lowered himself into the hidden tunnel that ran under the house and up through the cellar. Moments later, Rik was inside the house.

Cash

Every nerve in Cash's body screamed out for speed, but the situation called for silence. Being silent meant going slowly. He watched from his hiding spot as Travis in his filthy hound form made his way, boldly and openly, into the trees.

Travis had only gone a few steps when he was surrounded by other gangly demon dogs sniffing him suspiciously.

One of them stood in his path, nose-to-nose. "Who are you that you think you can walk in here without fear?" It growled at him threateningly. The speech was more guttural but Cash recognized every word. *We might speak the same language but that's as far as our resemblance goes,* Cash thought. He sniffed contemptuously, forgetting for a moment to stay unseen. Fortunately, the hounds were too interested in Travis to notice him.

Travis, who had been vibrating with rage and anticipation since arriving in Kelowna, was clearly in no mood to be bullied. In one smooth motion, he leapt and sank his teeth deep into the throat of his interrogator, killing him instantly.

Cash recoiled in amazement. He'd never imagined his cousin Travis could be so cold-blooded. The other Drenykin hounds seemed equally disturbed. They backed off eyeing Travis warily.

"Anyone else want to know who I am?" Travis sneered dangerously in the language of hounds. It seemed the rest of them were satisfied, when no one answered. Instead, they began to follow Travis as he continued on his way, bowing their heads in submission. Travis had killed the alpha male.

Cash eased himself out of his hiding place and slinked away from the scene of the violence. He knew Travis was heading for his mother. Cash's priority was finding Abby. He loped along silently, sniffing for a familiar scent that would lead him to Abby. The forest was vast. His heart pounded with urgency but his search was futile. He knew in his bones that Abby didn't come through the forest.

He was about to give up and head for the water when he caught a familiar scent. It was very faint. Cash would have missed it if he hadn't known the source. It was the scent of Sider apples and cinnamon. It was the scent of a certain elf.

Abby

The water was completely calm, which made Abby nervous. A little sloshing could cover sounds better. What if Uncle Rik got caught? What if Uncle Teej got caught? Abby, who was completely submerged, stopped herself and squeezed her eyes shut for a moment. She focused on calming her racing heart.

As she opened her eyes again, a ripple spread across the surface of the water above her. Abby peeked the top of her head out of the water and scanned the lake for boats. It was a quiet night. She could see the light coming from two boats across the lake. But they were too far away to cause ripples this size.

Abby listened carefully. Yes. There it was. A boat was approaching with no lights and no engine. Abby's heart began to race. This was the moment she had been dreading. This wasn't a game. This was war.

Determined not to let her uncles down, Abby took a deep breath and started with a soft hum. Her voice was incredible; like a sweet, brilliant caress. It carried poignantly over the increasing waves.

Abby continued to sing, locked now into the rhythm of her pounding heart. The words and melody came to her as naturally as a breeze on a lake. She sang of lovers separated, heartache and loss. Her beautiful song carried over the waves, seducing them into an increasing frenzy.

As it neared, the boat became more visible. Abby's voice continued to fill the lake and the air. The water began to swirl dangerously. The twisting waves made the boat tip violently from side to side. As her voice rose, so did the waves rise faster and faster in circles until the boat, too, began to spin.

Abby watched as her song fed the storm raging around her enemy. She could see the dark shape of a man, grasping desperately for a hold inside the small craft. Her voice rang out loudly for a final heart-stopping crescendo, flipping the boat and thrusting the man aboard it deep into the thrashing waters. Above the noise of the deafening waves and her own shrieking death-song, Abby did not hear him scream her name before he drowned.

Samantha

There was no chance to warn him. One moment they were cruising silently towards the house, side-by-side; she in the water, and he in the boat. The next moment, the air was filled with the most beautiful song she had ever heard and, within moments, a raging storm took them both by surprise. *Abby*. Samantha watched as Uncle Michael's lifeless body was thrown into the bottomless lake. If he was still alive, he wouldn't be for long.

She'd lost her arm attempting to save him; accidentally slipped it through the steering wheel while reaching for Michael. It had ripped right off. She winced with pain and regret. Would they both die in this lake? Her mouth filled with bloody water as she watched her uncle's body sink slowly into the depths.

Samantha began to lose consciousness when she suddenly felt herself being pushed back up to the surface of the water by something hard and scaly. Too weak and delirious to make sense of it, she succumbed to the darkness that beckoned her.

Jack

He waited quietly in his human form to avoid detection by his enemies. The cave his grandfather had chosen would only fit half of his dragon body. But it was spacious and deep in his human form. Before this day, Jack would have jumped at the opportunity to explore a cave such as this. But tonight, he focused on the task at hand.

"I guess I'm not a child anymore." The sound of his voice echoing in the dark opening of the cave made him feel even more alone. He thought about his mother who was also alone.

Jack's thoughts were suddenly interrupted by the frantic sound of flapping wings coming towards him. He prepared himself to change but before he could do it, Grandpa Torrents appeared in the air before him. He trilled eerily, landing on the cave floor, and phased into his human form before the sound finished echoing.

"Come now. Samantha is hurt. And…" Torrents' eyes darkened, as he hesitated.

"And what?" Jack barked anxiously.

"Your dad is barely alive."

"Where are they?" demanded Jack.

"They are with the lake beasts on the other side. We have to get them home as soon as possible."

Jack didn't have time to wonder what his grandfather meant by "the lake beasts." Grandpa Torrents was already running. Jack was right behind him. He took a flying leap off the edge of the cliff and phased mid-air into his dragon form. He followed his grandfather out over the lake. As they flew over the house, Jack could see Drenykin hellhounds running towards the water.

He spit fire, fighting an overpowering urge to swoop down and torch a few. Another time, he promised.

Abby

Shouting was coming from the shore. Her little windstorm had drawn attention. Abby stayed low in the waves so she would not be seen. Flashlights scanned the water around her but didn't find her. Then suddenly the voices grew louder.

"Right there!" A voice shouted. Abby's heart jumped. Could they see her? "Oh my God! It's the beast! *The beast!*" The man yelled. He and the other men on shore turned and ran towards the house. Abby was confused. *What beast?* Slowly, she turned around.

Above her loomed a large, snakelike creature with a towering neck and a large head, blinking long-lashed eyes. The creature was enormous but for some reason, Abby was not afraid.

"Come with me," it said, in a beautiful voice. "Come with me," it said again, sounding like a woman in love. Then it backed away. Abby was mesmerized. Her heart was filled with reverence for the amazing creature before her.

"Come with me, Abby." It sang seductively.

"But where are we going?" Abby asked.

"You're going home, Abby." The creature's sensuous voice hypnotized Abby.

Home. Gosh, Abby wanted to go home. To Cash. To her mom. She even missed Jack. Abby definitely wanted to go home. "Okay," she replied.

The serpent-creature led Abby across the lake, undulating through the waves, its scales glistening in the moonlight. They came to a secluded inlet. As they approached, Abby saw that they were not alone. Two other serpent-like lake beasts waited there for them. Abby recognized the area. The car was parked nearby.

"Thank you so much," Abby said to her escort. "I know where I am…"

"Abby?"

A hoarse but familiar voice interrupted her. Abby turned towards it. One of the lake beasts carried a passenger. She lay atop the beast, holding the bloody stump of an arm. It was her cousin.

"Sam! What happened?" Abby cried as she swam quickly to Samantha's side. "What are you doing here?" Tears sprang to her eyes. There was so much blood.

"I'm okay, Abby," Samantha smiled as she spoke. "Look." She held up her stump. "It's already growing back. It's one of my powers."

Abby was not relieved. "Who did this to you?"

Samantha's face grew grim. She didn't answer. It was almost midnight. The only noise was the sound of waves lapping gently against the beach. Then, fire in the night sky caught their attention.

"It's Jack and Grandpa Torrents!" Samantha exclaimed. "They'll be so happy to see you, Abby!"

Abby was in shock. What were they all doing here? Why was Sam injured? For the first time since she'd arrived at the inlet, Abby looked around at the beasts who congregated silently. Abby realized that there was another passenger laying prostate and pale on the hump of another lake beast. It looked like …

"Michael?" Abby said tentatively.

"Abby, you didn't know it was him," Samantha said quickly. "You couldn't have known."

Before Abby could make sense of what Samantha was saying, her griffin grandfather flew down and hovered above her. He chirped excitedly, landing beside Samantha on the back of the lake beast, then phased into his human form.

"Abby! Thank the Creator you are here," he said. "There is no time to waste. I'm going to fly your father up to Jack, then you can help Samantha onto my back. I will take you both."

"But…" Abby wanted to know what had happened. "Is he dead?"

Grandpa Torrents ignored her question. "We must hurry, Abby. The Drenykin are coming." He quickly phased back into his griffin form, lifting off to skim the lake. He grasped Michael gingerly with his claws and spiraled up into the sky. Moments later he returned for his granddaughters.

As they ascended into the dark, night sky, Abby looked back at the beautiful lake beasts who had saved them. But all that remained were three, fading, circular ripples on the surface of the water. "Goodbye," Abby whispered as her tears began to fall.

Rik

He didn't know whether to be worried or relieved when he heard the shouts of "the beast, the beast" coming from outside; worried that Abby had become fish food or relieved that she hadn't been seen by Drenykin warriors. Footsteps pounded past the closet where he hid. A door opened at the end of the hall and a familiar voice rang out.

"What's going on out here?"

"It's the sea beast, Jerematicus" said an excited voice. "It came up real close and gave old Danton a fright. Gave us all a fright," he explained.

Jerematicus sounded angry but interested. "First of all, it's a lake, not an ocean. So, it is not a sea beast," he spat. "Second of all, you should have killed it. Send some fliers out to see if they can find it. Put this lake monster non-sense to sleep, once and for all."

"Yes, Jerematicus," the other man agreed. "He caught us off-guard. And his fearsome nature is legendary."

"I have my own theory about the lake monster," Jerematicus said. "Can any of you draw? I'd like to see what he looked like." Their footsteps and voices faded away. The coast was clear for Rik to make his move.

He slipped out of the closet silently and walked with elf precision to the door at the end of the hallway. He knew Lacey was in there from the descriptions Abby had given him. He braced himself for danger, then quickly slipped inside.

They were alone.

Lacey was slumped in a chair, bound and gagged. Tubes stretched from both wrists ending in bags where her blood was collected, drip-by-drip.

As if she sensed he was there, she opened her eyes and stared at him. Her lips didn't move. It was her eyes that silently said "I'm dying." But Rik heard it like a shout, loud and clear.

"No," he whispered. But before he could go to her, the door opened behind him. Rik whipped around to face his opponent and came face-to-face with Cash. He pushed the door closed quickly.

"What are you doing here?" he demanded.

"Tell me where Abby is," Cash begged. His face was pale. He had deep circles under his eyes. He grabbed Rik by the shirt with both fists. "I need to find her."

"This is not the time, my friend," Rik replied. "Have you met my sister? She's dying over here. Help me get her out."

Rik slid the IV's out of his sister's wrists while Cash loosened her restraints. She fell into Rik's arms like a ragdoll. He hugged her close. "I'm here now, Lacey. I'm so sorry we took so long." He nodded towards the door.

"See if the coast is clear," he instructed Cash.

Cash opened the door a crack and peeked out with one eye. "Uh, that's a negative. There's three of 'em coming this way," he warned. He promptly turned into a wolf as the door swung in.

Rik had Lacey in his arms, which gave him only two options. Put her down and fight or surrender. At the moment, he could not bring himself to do either.

Three men came into the room, surprise registering on their faces as they took in the scene. The first one phased quickly into a massive black hellhound. He faced Cash, nose-to-nose, each baring his teeth viciously.

The second man grew suddenly into a giant. He stalked towards Rik menacingly with his hands held out like claws. Rik hugged Lacey to his chest and darted out of the way. His foot slammed hard into the giant's kneecap. The big man fell and Rik turned for the door.

But the doorway was blocked. It was Jerematicus — smiling that twisted, familiar smile that Rik had grown to loathe. It was the same grin he saw in his nightmares each night, with shining, checkerboard gold teeth and pitch white hair.

"Hello, Rik," he said icily. "It's a regular family reunion." His eyes glowed red as they bored into Rik's.

"You will not touch my sister again," Rik replied.

Travis

It was pure instincts that made him do it. And a healthy dose of killer rage, of course. Each time Travis took on someone else's powers, he gained their instincts, their ways of being for a short time. In the case of a hellhound, there was some evil in his ways.

His score was two for two. That was the second hellhound he'd killed. The first time, any feelings of guilt for committing murder were overshadowed by his elation at having joined the pack, or so he thought at the time. But this kill was different. This hound of hell had stood between Travis and his mother. A mistake he shouldn't have made.

Now, Travis led the pack. Such irony. Unfortunately, the Drenykin captain who guarded his mother had brought his own protection. The slovenly, pampered mutts that guarded the house didn't have a real pack leader. They followed the Drenykin captain.

Travis so longed to meet this Drenykin captain. And rip his throat out.

In the meantime, his main concern was keeping his subordinates loyal. If they suspected he was a Fatum imposter, they would kill him.

He played the role of guarding the house and protecting the property. But he spent his time learning the layout of the land. He didn't know how he was going to do it. But he'd already made it this far. And he wasn't leaving without his mother.

Abby

Returning home felt like a dream. The faces of her loved ones were fuzzy and indistinct. Abby was exhausted. Samantha had explained what happened while they flew. Abby cried in remorse. By the time they landed, Abby was numb.

She allowed herself to be hugged and loved on repeatedly by different members of her family. She heard the words many times … *that it was not her fault.*

She saw her mother's relief when Abby arrived and her grief when her eyes settled on Michael. But the numbness held. She felt nothing as her mother fell on Michael's lifeless body, weeping brokenly. After sharing everything she knew about her uncles with Grandpa Torrents and Uncle Duke, Abby found her bed.

She hoped she'd feel better tomorrow when she saw Cash. For a moment, at the thought of Cash, tears stung her eyes and she thought her emotions were returning to her. But no. They were gone again. The only thing Abby felt was a pounding headache. "Good night," she said to the empty night. She closed her eyes and fell asleep.

PART FIVE

RESURRECTION

Nurse your offspring on the sacred fruit of the Great Tree
to arm them with protection from your enemies.
Every generation will yield a Chosen One
who will lead The Cause.

Jack

Anguish was a hard emotion for a dragon to handle. Jack was unable to resume his natural form. He'd carried his father's cold body on his back for many miles. The man did not have life left in him. Jack could not be sure what good reason there was to be carrying him back to the house dead. He wished his own heart were dead, the pain was so great.

He erupted with a fresh howl, shooting flames from his nostrils as he struggled to control himself. Fatum warriors kept back for the most part, rushing in with hoses and buckets of water whenever his flames inadvertently started a fire. Jack should have felt bad putting others out like he was. But there was no room for shame in his heart. Only anguish.

All Jack knew was that his dead father was inside the house. And Jack wasn't letting anyone near him. He gnashed his teeth and let out a terror-striking scream. Again, he bathed the yard in fire. The grass surrounding the house was gone, serving as a visible line that no one dared to cross.

It was not enough to stalk around or circle the house from the sky. Jack found himself compelled to perch atop the roof, caving it in in several places. The destruction he was capable of had no end. But none of that mattered. His father was dead.

Duke

He wasn't surprised that Rik's plan had turned into a big family drama. It was a bold plan. In Duke's opinion, it was a foolish plan.

But Duke had been wrong before. Sometimes he thought Rik had the Creator in his pocket. Especially when seemingly crazy ideas turned out to be true winners. Or when he survived battles he shouldn't have survived. Duke hoped this would be one of those times, when Rik's genius overcame his impulsiveness. And even though all hell had broken loose, there was still a chance that Rik's plan might work.

The closer family members congregated inside the house. Jack's willful presence on the roof prevented any others. Which was just as well, since private decisions were being made. Decisions that would not be shared with the rest of the force camping on the grounds.

Like Julea's decision. She'd wept over Michael's body for a long time before raising resigned eyes. "I'm doing it," she said. No one argued. Duke helped Uncle Torrents move Michael's lifeless body to the bed.

"You're taking a big risk," Aunt Dianna said. "What if you lose the baby?"

"She will need a father," Julea replied. Duke could tell she'd made up her mind and nothing was going to change it. Aunt Dianna persisted.

"Julea, please reconsider. If the Elders find out, you might be punished."

"I am willing to take that chance," Julea said.

Duke wanted to comfort her. "I will deal with anyone who says a word about this, myself," he promised. Julea smiled weakly at him and squeezed his hand.

"Thank you, Duke," she said.

She went to the kitchen and returned with a sharp knife. "Can you hold his mouth open, Duke?"

"Of course," he replied. He watched as she held the knife over a candle flame, sterilizing both sides. He turned his head when she drew the knife across her palm. He wasn't afraid of blood. He just found it hard to watch her hurt herself.

"It's okay," she whispered. "It doesn't hurt as much as the thought of losing him forever."

Duke held Michael's mouth open for Julea. She began to hum, while she administered her blood to his mouth. Drip, drip, drip. It was a full two hours before Michael stirred. They continued well into the morning. Michael grew stronger and Julea grew weaker.

A few hours after sunrise, Teej returned. He came straight to Julea's bedroom to offer consolation and share information. After watching the house all night, Teej had returned empty handed. He reported that Rik went in but did not come out.

Julea wasn't administering her blood to Michael anymore. Now she wrapped her body around his and spoke softly. If Duke didn't know any better, he'd think she didn't want to wake him. But truthfully, she was spent. Every word required effort.

"Jerematicus will torture him again," she said quietly.

"Not necessarily," Teej replied. "Rik was caught off guard when they attacked him last time. This time he won't hold anything back."

"That's true," agreed Duke. "Rik is a wicked scrapper, never mind his poisonous spit."

They shared an uneasy laugh. Rik had melted many things with his toxic saliva.

Michael still lay unconscious, but his breathing was steady. It would take time for Julea's blood to do its work inside his body. Whether he would make a full recovery remained to be seen.

Teej seemed to be reading Duke's mind. "So, Sis," he said. "What's the prognosis? Will Michael be building toys in no time? Or is a full recovery too much to expect?"

"I've never done this before," Julea admitted. Her voice was hoarse. "The most I ever did outside of battle was hide a drop in a glass of juice when one of the kids was sick. Lacey and I both had it drilled relentlessly into our heads that Unicorn blood is for healing. Never resurrecting. I think the fact that such a rare power showed up in two females of the same family really freaked the Elders out. Nothing about it was mentioned in the Prophecy. But something like this couldn't be a coincidence. It's like the Elders knew the Creator favoured us, so they wanted to make sure we didn't screw up." She sighed.

"Do you want another glass of water, Julea?" Duke asked, rising slightly from his chair.

"No, I'm fine, Duke. But thank you. I know what I've done is wrong. But it feels right. I have no idea what will happen to Michael. I gave him much more blood than

I've ever administered to anyone. After he took his first few breaths, I continued to nurse him through the night. I couldn't stop myself. Only time will tell if it was enough. Or too much, for that matter. In the meantime, I have a new concern. The child inside of me is suffering. I may lose her. Creator help me if I lose them both."

"You won't," Duke assured her, though he had no way of keeping such a promise. It was in the Creator's hands now. His thoughts were interrupted by a loud voice in the house.

"Julea! Julea!"

"It's Angus," Julea said. She dragged herself up. Teej rushed over to support her, but the door opened before she took a step.

Angus' large frame filled the doorway. "I would have been here sooner but your son doesn't acknowledge my rank. Seemed to think I deserved to have my beard burned off." Angus' singed whiskers still smoked. "Where are Cash and Travis?" he asked. "Have they returned with the others?"

Uncle Torrents had followed him in. "No, they did not," he informed Angus. "They were on the ground when the accident happened. We have no idea if they've been taken or not."

"Maybe we should ask Abby," Teej suggested quietly.

"What do you mean?" Torrents asked. "How would Abby know? She told us everything that happened. She didn't mention Cash or Travis at all."

Teej looked at Angus penetratingly, as if unsure whether he should share what he wanted to say with someone outside the family. He shrugged his shoulders resignedly.

"Lacey's been sending Abby visions," he said.

Duke felt the words like a punch in the stomach. He watched as Julea, who'd been leaning heavily on her brother, straightened suddenly. Her voice, only a whisper before, became loud and hoarse. "What?" She grabbed Teej by the shirt with both hands and stared up into his face. "Tell me it isn't true," she begged.

"I'm so sorry, Sis," Teej said. "But it's true. It's true."

Julea's face drained of colour. As her knees buckled, Duke and Teej caught her between them. Teej lifted his unconscious sister into his arms, while Duke pulled back the bedspread.

"This cannot be good for the baby," Duke murmured. Teej made a grunt of agreement as he laid Julea down beside Michael. She was already coming out of her faint.

"I don't think I can walk, but please take me to Abby," she said.

"Of course," Teej replied. He carried her to Abby's room.

Duke pulled up a chair beside Abby's bed and offered it to Julea. The room was hot, bathed in the warm glow of the mid-morning sun. One bright ray shone through the window, resting on Abby's peaceful, sleeping face.

The blatant sign from the Creator must have startled Julea, because she suddenly began shaking Abby violently. "Abby, Abby! Wake up!" she said desperately. Duke started to reach for Julea to stop her. Then he realized why Julea was freaking out.

Abby wasn't waking up.

Rik

Jerematicus smiled menacingly at Rik. "You must be mistaking me for someone else," he said. "I don't take orders from elves."

"She's dying," Rik replied. "Are you prepared to endure her curse? My sister can be very creative."

The giant had pulled himself to his feet. He advanced towards Rik. But Rik was faster. He aimed his spit at the center of the giant's left eye. *Thhhpoof!* The large man howled in agony as he reached for his face.

"Oops," said Jerematicus. "I should have warned you about that. His saliva is toxic so don't get too close." Rik had backed himself into a corner. He still carried Lacey's limp body in his arms. Cash stood in front of him growling viciously. Jerematicus remained blocking the doorway, a Drenykin hound at his side. The giant continued to wail loudly.

"Oh, shut up," Jerematicus said suddenly. In one smooth motion, he pulled his long sword from its scabbard and cut off the giant's head. It rolled across the floor towards Jerematicus' feet. He kicked it aside, sneering distastefully at the blood as he turned his eyes back to Rik, and the wolf and hellhound facing off between them.

"Now, where were we?" he said mockingly.

"I'm serious," Rik said. "She's dying. You can believe me and save yourself. Or you can take your chances. But she told me she was dying. And you know a unicorn can't lie."

For the first time, Jerematicus seemed concerned. "She spoke to you? We haven't heard her speak for days. I don't believe you."

"I am her brother. We don't need words to communicate," Rik replied angrily. "If she wasn't my sister, I'd let her die just so I could watch you suffer the curse," he added. As he said the words, Rik had an epiphany. That's what the Elders were doing with Lacey. They were sacrificing one Fatum for the demise of this Drenykin trash.

"Don't you wonder why the Elders didn't attack when Lacey's capture was so conveniently leaked?" Rik asked.

"That was my idea," Jerematicus admitted. "I'd hoped to lure you back. The games we played last time we were together were so much fun. I have to admit, I was surprised when all you did was watch us by yourself for so long. I remember unicorns to be sacred among you bleeding-heart Fatums. Tell me. Why didn't the Elder's attack?"

Rik hardened his emotions against Jerematicus' taunts.

"They were willing to sacrifice Lacey to cripple you."

Jerematicus raised his eyebrows. "How malicious," he observed. "I didn't think the Fatum had it in them," he sneered. But Rik could see he was considering his words carefully.

"Very well, then," Jerematicus said decidedly. "Nurse your sister back to health. Food and water will be provided for her and her only. My guards will ensure my conditions are obeyed. Know that this only delays your demise, Rik Sider. Revive your sister so she can watch me kill you. It's much more fun with an audience," he rubbed his hands together wickedly.

Julea

Abby's bed was moved to Julea's bedroom. Julea hummed softly as she cared for her slumbering husband and daughter. Michael slept peacefully, but Abby stirred often, mumbling unintelligibly.

Julea dripped broth from a cloth into their mouths. She washed faces and smoothed hair. She poured love on them as much as she could, hoping her love energy would wake them. Her mother urged her to take a break. For the baby.

Julea didn't tell her mother, but the baby was already gone. Julea hadn't felt any movement since the wee hours of the morning. Even more telling was the return of her compulsion to fight. Something a Fatum mother doesn't experience until all of her living children have received their powers. No. The baby must be gone. Julea would mourn later. There was much to do right now. One life was lost, but there were still three lives to save.

Cash

He knew he was no match for the large hound. Cash was just a pup compared to the massive beast towering over him. He stood his ground anyway. If he was going down, he would go down fighting.

When the white-haired Drenykin gave Rik permission to care for Lacey, he also spared Cash's life. "You can keep your dog for now," he said mockingly. "He will report your death back to your mother for me."

Cash growled in response causing Rik to laugh aloud.

"I don't think he likes you," Rik said.

"He just doesn't know me," Jerematicus replied.

Several more hounds were called to the room to guard the Fatum warriors. Cash's eyes watered. "Torture by stench," he muttered. The hounds growled menacingly in unison.

"Hey, take it easy," Rik said, as he made a makeshift bed on the floor for Lacey. "Come lie against my sister and keep her warm." Cash obeyed his command. Her body was cold. He licked her face worriedly.

Rik organized Lacey with blankets supplied by the Drenykin. They brought water and broth too, as promised. The smell of the food made Cash's stomach growl loudly.

"Don't eat anything," Rik warned quietly. "Those hounds are hoping for an excuse to annihilate us." Cash nodded understanding.

Rik sat against the wall with Lacey's head on his lap. Cash laid the length of her body, lending his body heat.

They remained that way for hours; Rik administering broth to Lacey's lips in small amounts. Cash became increasingly agitated. Being apart from Abby for so long was hurting him. It was like having his breath stolen from him. He was also very hungry. He began to feel desperate and his hair stood on end.

Rik must have sensed his desperation. "Don't attempt anything," he whispered. "We must save Lacey."

Cash was beginning to agree with the Elders. What was one life if it defeated this monster? Her death could provide the means for their escape. Escape would mean food and Abby. Two things Cash needed more than anything right now.

"Cash, listen to me," Rik whispered again. "I know what you're probably thinking. But I'm going to tell you something that will change your mind drastically. We must save Lacey, because if she dies, our mutual loved one will die too."

Cash was confused. He considered phasing into his human form so he could speak openly. He didn't have to because Rik explained.

"My sister did something very dangerous," Rik whispered. "She linked her fate with this person we both love so she could send her visions to help us find her. The problem is, the link is permanent. If Lacey dies, the person we love will die too."

It took Cash a moment to understand. Rik wasn't saying her name because he was protecting her. But there was only one person that both Rik and Cash loved. *Abby.*

Jack

Grandpa Torrents delivered the message. "It's time to go inside," he said gently. "There are no dead to protect anymore. Your father is alive, though barely. But there is reason for hope."

Jack phased into his human form. They sat beside each other on the broken roof of the house. "How can this be?" Jack asked. "My father was dead. I carried him back. I know he was dead."

Torrents looked around for nearby listeners, but most of their family members and fellow warriors continued to keep their distance from Jack. Torrents spoke quietly. "Your mother's supernatural form is a unicorn. Her blood has amazing healing powers. However, it is against Fatum law to resurrect a person. That is why we were so relieved that your dad was still alive when we got here." His eyes bored into Jack's. "He was still alive, but barely. Your mother was able to stabilize him with her blood. He is unconscious still, but his heartbeat is strong. We do not yet know for sure if he will fully recover."

Jack got the picture. Mom had broken the law and resurrected his father. He would be expected to lie about his father's injury to protect his mother.

"Maybe you're right," he said. "I was very tired and worried. I suppose he could have still been alive."

Grandpa Torrents smiled. "That's my boy," he said. "There is one other thing I have to tell you though. Your sister is ill. Jack, your mother needs you inside."

Jack looked around at the burnt lawn and hastily moved tents. He wondered how many fires his comrades had put out because of him during the night. "I'm a little embarrassed," he said, nodding towards the devastation.

"Oh, don't you worry about that, Buds," Grandpa Torrents said flippantly. "Dragons have been around for a long time. It's your instinct to protect the injured and dead. You should have seen your Uncle Duke the first time Darla was injured in battle. That's one of the reasons he stopped drinking. I wonder what he's going to be like when Lyll brings home a scratch or two. I shudder to imagine." He smiled kindly at Jack.

"Uncle Duke is a dragon? Why didn't anyone tell me?" Jack asked.

"Oh, you would have found out sooner or later. Most of us are so used to our supernatural forms, we don't think to bring it up in conversation anymore. But we all remember how fun those early days were when we were just learning our powers."

"Alright. Thanks Grandpa Torrents," Jack replied. "Should we jump down, then?"

"I don't know about you, but I like to take opportunities as they arise. And this is a perfect opportunity to practice our back flips." Grandpa Torrents chuckled as he stood on the edge of the roof with his back to the ground. He bent his knees briefly, before sailing backwards off the roof. He landed gracefully on the ground and looked up at Jack.

"Your turn," he said. "Show me what you got."

Rising to the challenge, Jack couldn't help but show a little arrogance at a moment like this. "You ain't seen nothing yet, Old Man," he replied. He jumped into the air, and breathing a ring of fire as he went, he pulled off three rotations before landing like a pro next to his grandfather.

"Show off," Grandpa Torrents teased. They entered the house together smiling.

Travis

Travis prowled the property learning as much as he could about his enemy and the location of his mother. The hounds that guarded the house gave regular reports to his pack. Travis learned that Rik and Cash were inside with his mother, being guarded by several Drenykin hounds. It became Travis' sole goal to become one of those guards.

It wouldn't be easy. Travis' predecessor didn't get along with the "house pets" — a nickname Travis learned from his pack members. Those who made up Jerematicus' personal guard did not trust the hounds that protected the property. Since they didn't comingle, Travis' new presence as pack leader didn't even faze them. He was as unfamiliar as the rest of them.

The house pets knew that Travis had killed their nemesis, for that is the only way to become a pack leader among hellhounds. Perhaps that was why they didn't attack Travis when they first met him. Whatever it was, Travis intended to use it to his advantage. Somehow, some way, he was going to get into the house as a guard. Then he would reassess and make his next move.

Abby

She could feel herself slowly easing into consciousness. A blinking light blinded her till she realized it was her eyes opening and closing. She was still in prison. She heard a voice and became aware that someone held her.

"It's okay, Darling," the voice said. "I'm here. I'm taking care of you. You're going to be alright."

She turned her head painfully towards the voice, looking into the kind face of Uncle Rik. Relief flooded her veins. She tried to say thank you but the effort drained her. Everything faded to black again, including the pain. She was grateful for that.

Teej

He listened to Grandma Rose rage on her son, Torrents, and suffered through the comments directed at himself. She cursed Rik and Lacey, and frequently cast suspicious glances towards Julea. Dad took it like a man.

"I know, Mom," Torrents soothed repeatedly until she calmed down a bit. "What's done is done. So, let's talk now about how we're going to fix it."

"Well, I'll tell you how we're going to fix it," she replied. "We're going to walk in that house, slap Jerematicus silly, and take our loved ones home. Then, when they're feeling recovered enough from their experiences, we're going to punish them so bad they'll wish Jerematicus still had them!"

Teej held in a laugh. His grandma was so feisty. And boy, did she have a temper. No one dared to speak when she was in a tirade other than Dad.

"Grandma, are you suggesting that we launch another private mission? Because if so, then you'll be getting punished alongside us," Julea quipped. *I stand corrected,* Teej thought. My sister is as crazy as old pops.

Grandma Rose looked at Julea sadly. "No. We will have the full support of the Elders," she said. "I must tell them about Abby immediately. They…we will not allow the Final Chosen One to be jeopardized as you all have."

She walked angrily towards the door, but instead of reaching for the handle, she flipped her wrist dramatically. The door exploded outwards in a shower of splinters. She stalked out kicking debris as she went.

"Whoa, Grandma is really mad," Teej observed.

"She'll get over it," Torrents replied. "We've got some other decisions to make now. Like, who is going to stay behind with Julea?"

"Dad, I'm okay. I don't need anyone…" Julea was interrupted by Torrents.

"No, Julea. It's not just about you. The Elders will leave warriors behind to protect Abby. I'd feel more comfortable if we had some family members as well."

Teej listened quietly while his parents, aunts, uncles, and cousins discussed who would be going and who would be staying behind. He knew he wouldn't be staying behind. No one would expect him to, with two siblings to account for. Lacey was clearly dying. One look at Abby could tell you that.

Well, all Teej knew was that Rik had found a way into the house and entered it. His mockingbird call being the last Teej had heard from him.

Julea was also quiet. Just as it was clearly obvious why Teej was going, it was clearly obvious why she was staying. Teej knew that under different circumstances, his sister would be one of the deadliest fighters in the fray. He didn't imagine that motherhood had softened her battle skills. If anything, she was probably more vicious now that her own children were fighting. But she was pregnant, and her husband and daughter both lay unconscious here.

Presently, Grandma Rose returned. "The Final Fire will be held tonight. We will leave directly after."

"Wait," Jack whispered to Teej. "Is Grandma Rose coming too?" he asked incredulously.

Teej laughed quietly. "Hehe, you are in for a real eye opener, my man," he said. "Grandma could beat you around the block anytime."

Jack did not look amused, which made Teej laugh harder. He clapped his nephew on the back. "Don't worry," he said. "I have faith in you. Tonight, we're going to kick some butt together. You, me, and Grandma Rose."

Rik

Relieved to see that Lacey was improving, if slightly, Rik started to pay more attention to his guards. The hounds usually remained in their dog forms, but occasionally they would enter the room before making the change. He memorized their faces.

Rik might know well a hellhound he has seen many times. But the same hound could walk past him in the street in his human form, and Rik wouldn't recognize him at all. He could only hope that the smell would give the impostor away.

It was the luck of the draw. Some Fatum and Drenykin had the same advantage. They looked completely different from one form to the other, like Jack in his dragon form. Elves, like Rik however, looked much the same in both their forms. The word 'incognito' would never be used to describe him.

By the light from the barred window, Rik could tell it was late in the day. If he'd arrived any later, Lacey would probably be dead. *Thank you, Creator,* Rik prayed silently. *Now, could you please get us out of here?*

Rik smiled. He knew better than to expect the Creator to do things his way. Whatever destiny had in store; it wouldn't involve making an easy retreat. Rik estimated that the Elders would be sending in the Faery Corps sometime soon.

In the end, he hadn't even needed to bring Abby along, he realized. Lacey had involved her more than Rik could have even imagined. Rik respected her for it. She must have realized that the Elders were sacrificing her and done what she needed to do to survive. She linked her fate to the Final Chosen One. Gutsy, controversial, and bold. Three words that described his sister, Lacey, perfectly.

It was good to have her back. Even if it was behind enemy lines.

Lacey began to stir again. She seemed stronger as her muscles tensed and she braced herself to rise.

"Hey, hey, hey, relax, Sista," Rik said quickly, persuading her not to move.

"Rik," she breathed, staring up at him. She looked around frantically. As she turned, she came face to face with Cash. Her eyes grew round with horror. "What are you doing here?" she whispered urgently.

Cash whimpered and cocked his head at her.

"It's okay, Lacey," Rik tried to soothe her. "He's with us. Calm down and I'll explain everything to you."

"Has the Sacred One recovered?" Jerematicus' voice intruded rudely, as he entered the room.

Rik helped Lacey to a sitting position against the wall and stood up. "I wouldn't say she has recovered. It seems her life might be prolonged a little more. But, if you use her badly again, I can't promise she'll endure."

"Do not worry, Rik Sider. I have no desire to tempt a curse. This is only one assignment, after all. I am but one jailkeeper. No. It is not my intention to take more of her blood. We have banks of it already. Three years is a long time to be draining a unicorn. Come to think of it, I'm surprised she lasted as long as she did." He paused, turning assessing eyes on Lacey. "I can see she is still weak. I will wait till she's a bit stronger, so I can be sure she won't have a heart attack or anything tragic like that. Then I will kill you and send your slinking dog home. Your sister will remain a Drenykin Prisoner of War as though nothing has changed; your bumbling effort a shameful last act for your family to remember you by."

Rik shrugged his shoulders disinterestedly. "Bring it on, JJ." He turned and spit on the hound closest to him. The room filled with alternating yelps and shrieks, as the hound seemed undecided about which form would best serve him in the moment. The other hounds jumped to their feet, growling. Cash, too, bared his teeth menacingly, placing himself in front of Lacey.

"Enough," Jerematicus ordered to no one in particular. The hounds backed off regretfully. Cash kept his position, his fur standing on end, fangs bared, saliva dripping from his mouth.

Rik was aware of his sister's tense energy, yet he jumped when she suddenly cried out. Her voice startled him, as well as the name she called out. For it was Abby's voice. And the name she called out was: *"Cash!"*

Julea

"Cash!" Abby cried as she sat up, her face full of horror.

"What is it, Angel?" Julea asked, rushing to her daughter's side, and pulling her into her arms. Abby gasped for air. Tears streamed down her face.

"What is he doing there?" she asked frantically.

"What did you see, Baby Girl?" Julea asked softly, attempting to calm her. "Did you see Cash?"

"Yes. I saw him. But it can't be. He's here at home. Isn't he, Mama? My nightmares are getting mixed up with my visions, right Mama?" Abby's eyes pleaded with her mother.

Julea wanted to comfort her but a unicorn cannot lie. "No Baby. Cash went looking for you. He hasn't returned yet."

"Oh no!" Abby burst into fresh tears, sobbing against her mother. Her sobs subsided suddenly.

"Well, we must go get him," Abby declared, making to rise out of bed. "We must get him before he is hurt or killed!"

Julea restrained Abby forcefully in her embrace. "No," she commanded gently. "You must rest until you are stronger. I will summon my brother so you can tell him everything you know. We strike tonight after the Final Fire of the Elders."

Julea was relieved as Abby settled down, at least for the moment. She went to the door and called for Teej.

"Abby has regained consciousness," she said when he arrived. "She has some information to share that will aid our mission tonight."

"Abby, what a relief to see you up and talking. We were very worried about you," Teej said as he sat in the chair beside her bed.

"Why?" Abby asked. "In fact, why am I in this room. What is going on?"

"You were unconscious, Abby," Teej explained. "The visions you are receiving from Lacey…well, they are more than just visions. She has linked herself to you."

Abby was nodding her head. "Yes," she said. "It is more. I feel her pain, her fear. I feel her anger. And something else. Um, it's like regret. Like she's losing hope and having regrets." Abby held her stomach in demonstration.

"I'm not surprised," Teej replied. "She likely regrets putting this enchantment on you, Abby."

"But it is good that she has!" Abby argued. "I was able to give you and Uncle Rik lots of important information about where she was. And I have even more to tell you, Uncle Teej! Rik is with Lacey now. And Cash is there too. They are surrounded by Drenykin hounds…"

"Your help has been invaluable, for sure, Abby," Teej replied patiently. "And I want to hear more about Lacey. But first, we need to talk about the enchantment. The link that Lacey has imposed on you is very dangerous. Because if Lacey dies…" He hesitated for a moment. "…if Lacey dies, you will die too. It is the nature of such enchantments."

Teej's last words trailed off. Julea stepped behind him and placed her hand on his shoulder.

"We cannot know for sure why my sister joined her fate with yours, Baby Girl," Julea said. "She could not have known…about you. And your importance to The Cause."

"My importance to The Cause?"

Julea was distressed to be discussing such serious topics when Abby had just regained consciousness. But these were things that needed to be said. And after all, Abby was asking.

"Abby, listen to me," Julea began. "I should have told you sooner, but I wanted you to have some time before you had the weight of the world on your shoulders. But now, I hope that it will in some way comfort you to know why the Fatum forces are going to do everything in their power to save Lacey."

"What, Mama? What are you talking about?" Abby asked tearfully. The poor girl had been through so much in such a short time. Her innocence had been stolen so quickly. Julea's heart ached for her daughter deeply.

"Angel, you know how I said when you were born, you saved me?"

"Yes," Abby replied. "You said you were sad and feeling lost in the world, and then I came along and gave you a reason to live." These words Julea had often repeated over the years.

"Exactly," Julea smiled. "Well, it seems you were sent here to save more people than just me, Angel. Abby, you are the Chosen One. The Final Chosen One. The One we have all been waiting for. You will lead our Cause, Abby. And for that reason alone, the Elders will order Lacey saved immediately."

Abby was quiet. Julea watched the emotions play across Abby's face. Consternation etched her daughter's features. Finally, she spoke.

"That's good," she said. "But who will save Cash?"

"You don't worry about that," Teej declared. "It seems to me that Cash can hold his own. And we will be right there to back him up. Your young man is also very important to The Cause. We're not going to let anything happen to him if we can help it."

"Thank you," replied Abby. She hugged Teej. Then she told them everything she could remember.

Jack

"Come here, Jack," Grandma Rose said, crooking her finger at him. He approached her obediently. "Can you breathe some life into this pile of sticks, please?"

"Uh, sure Grandma," he replied. He leaned over and blew softly on the kindling. It began to burn readily. The ability to breathe fire was one of the powers he still had in his human form. Jack added some larger logs to the blaze.

"Thank you, Jack," Grandma squeezed him fondly. "You're a good boy," she said.

Jack blushed slightly. He didn't feel like a "good boy" when he saw the damage he'd done.

As Grandma Rose took her position, Jack looked at the faces surrounding them. Most he had barely met. Some were his closest friends and family members. He nodded at the McAllisters. They looked strange standing there without Cash and Travis. The expressions they wore were haunted, determined ones. For a moment, Jack felt ashamed that he was here while Cash and Travis had been left behind.

Abby's visions told them the fate of Cash and Rik. But Travis was unaccounted for. Jack chose to believe that Travis was alive and well, concocting a plan to rescue his mother as they spoke.

Grandma Rose cleared her throat. She began talking before everyone had quieted down. It had the effect of silencing them faster. No one wanted to miss her words. Especially tonight, when some of their own were in danger and the reunion was being interrupted by an important mission.

"You gathered here tonight wondering why you are called to arms only partway into our annual reunion," Rose began. She looked around for a moment before continuing. "I can assure you; this mission is of utmost importance. In a moment, you will understand why.

"I had planned to share the news with everyone during the Final Fire two days hence. Glorious and terrible news. As you are all aware, The End Times that were prophesied are now upon us. The signs arrived late last year when 'winged darkness' in the form of hundreds of crows, descended on the headquarters of every Fatum and Drenykin commune on Mother Earth.

"We all waited with bated breath to find out who would be the Final Chosen One, praying it would not be one of our own. Our commune has been both blessed, and some may say cursed, to have provided many of the Chosen for our long Cause. For many of you, it may be a great disappointment to realize that our efforts were in vain. We did not prevent the End Times from occurring. We've lost many lives to a Cause that seems doomed. A lost Cause, as our Drenykin brethren would, and often have declared of our work.

"I would be untruthful if I said I don't have the same doubts as some of you," Rose admitted. Jack wondered if this was the part where she would tell them that they were right. It *was* a lost Cause.

"I have been around a long, long time and there is one thing I have learned," she said. "I have learned that everything happens for a good reason. Even if what is happening is bad.

"Tonight, I'd like to introduce you all to the Final Chosen One. She has already proven herself courageous, compassionate, and deadly. Please show your respect for my great granddaughter, Abby Sider."

Abby

When Abby first woke, she did not notice her stepfather in the bed beside hers. She stared hard at him. "He isn't dead," she stated woodenly. Julea walked towards her and sat in the chair beside the bed.

"No," Julia replied. Her mother was quiet for a moment before confessing what she had done. "I broke the law. I gave him my blood," she whispered. "I resurrected him." Julea's eyes pleaded for Abby's understanding. "I couldn't help it."

"It's okay," Abby tried to comfort her. "He is your husband. Of course, you did…"

"There's more," Julea interrupted. "I was pregnant. I'm sorry I didn't tell you yet, Baby Girl, but I wanted this time to be yours and Jack's. I didn't want the baby distracting us all, this being your Sacred Summer."

"You're pregnant?" Abby grinned from ear-to-ear. But the look on her mother's face stopped her. "What Mama?"

Tears streamed down Julea's face. "I lost the baby. Well, she's still in there. But she hasn't moved for over twelve hours. And I…I can't feel her anymore."

"But maybe you're wrong, Mama," Abby insisted. She couldn't bear to see her mother so sad. "Maybe she's turned in a different position." Abby watched as a change come over her mother. Julea wiped her eyes, inhaled deeply, and forced a weak smile.

"You could be right," she said. Her eyes told Abby she didn't believe her own words.

Abby felt her lip tremble. "Oh Mom," she cried out. She threw her arms up over her face and burst into tears. "It's all my fault," she sobbed. "I'm horrible! I made this happen!"

"What are you talking about, Abby? It's not your fault," Julea insisted.

"If I hadn't used my powers to sink Michael's boat, you wouldn't have had to save him and the baby would be okay," Abby wailed. She couldn't help it. The reality of the situation hit her hard and fast. She hated herself. She had caused two deaths. Her baby sister…

"No, Baby Girl," Julea soothed. "It wasn't your fault. You did what you were instructed by your leader. And you did it very well. I am proud of you, Angel. You are smart, beautiful, and fierce. You should be proud of yourself too.

You are not the first Fatum to kill on her first mission, you know."

Abby became curious. "What do you mean, Mama? Who else …?"

"You look at me and see your mother who has loved and nurtured you your entire life," Julea said. "But you should know that I have killed too. I'm not saying it because I am proud. I want you to understand. As Fatum, we were born to this Cause. A part of our destiny involves war. There is only one way to win a war that I know of. That is to fight with all of your might. You will lead us in the battle. You are the Chosen One because you hold great power. Embrace it. Own it."

Abby listened intently. It was strange to hear her mom encouraging her to be violent. Abby looked back on her life. She realized that it wasn't the first time her mother had talked like this. Abby was raised with the philosophy that you should be kind to everyone, unless they were unkind to you. Even then, be kind but keep your distance. If anyone dared to physically or verbally assault you … Stand up for yourself. *Fight back.*

Julea's instructions had always irked Michael. He disagreed and scolded Julea for "teaching the kids such things." But Julea wouldn't back down. "You can't always be nice," she said firmly. "That's how people take advantage of you. Sometimes you have to set boundaries. Like 'back off before I punch you in the face.'"

Abby remembered giggling as Michael stormed out of the room. Okay, Abby realized, this attitude wasn't really new. Julea had always encouraged them to fight their own battles, with fists when necessary.

Both Abby and her mother were quiet, looking into each other's eyes. "You have lost your innocence, Abby. But you are not lost. I won't let you be."

Abby sniffed and wiped her eyes. "Thank you, Mama," she whispered.

Teej

The fire seemed to blaze higher as the crowd pressed closer to hear the Final Chosen One speak. Abby stood before the hushed faces filled with awe. Although most family members and some tree nymphs already knew, most of the Fatum gathered were surprised.

Abby was The One. The One who would lead The Cause until The End ... when the Earth Mother would either begin her restoration or be destroyed beyond repair. A young Fatum girl with the weight of the world on her shoulders. This day of nightmares had truly arrived.

Teej pitied her as she stood before their collective gaze. He spoke from his gut, loud and firm. "I see you, Abby Sider, Final Chosen One," he bowed low. "I will follow you till The End." He remained on one knee; his head bowed; his loyalty for all to witness.

Duke knelt next. The others followed. One-by-one, every member of the congregation fell on bended knee and pledged allegiance to Abby.

Teej watched with pride. She stood tall, with no trace of fear. She said the words he taught her before the Fire.

"I accept my destiny and devote my life to The Cause in service of our Blessed Creator."

The following silence was broken when a voice from the crowd asked, "And who is her Appointed Protector?" Teej turned to see who had spoken. It was young Cathryn McAllister. She'd clearly already made the connection and wanted to ensure her brother got his due.

"Thank you, Cathryn," Grandma Rose acknowledged. "Abby's Appointed Protector is Cash McAllister. At the moment of their first kiss, the crows left our lands. This being the final and irrevocable sign that these are indeed the End Times. Cash is a skilled and fierce warrior. The Creator blessed us when he chose Cash." Crowd members shuffled and strained to see Cash, wondering where he was.

Grandma Rose looked around. She bowed low to Abby before speaking again. "Under normal circumstances, the Final Fire of the Elders is a meeting of intelligence and strategy. But tonight, we are called to war. I will give you the facts but I beg you to withhold judgment. You will not be happy to hear what I tell you.

"Lacey Lynn Ryked, as many of you know, has been missing for almost three years. The Drenykin prize, above everything, the taking of a unicorn; for her blood has the power to heal. Our intelligence suggests to us that this is exactly what Lacey Lynn has been used for during her time in captivity. She has literally been drained of her blood. We also believe this was part of a malicious vendetta against certain members of our commune ...

"Fearing her life near the end, Lacey joined her fate with Abby Sider and began sending her visions." A collective gasp ran through the crowd. Teej felt a stab of anger that anyone might judge his sister for her actions. But even he had a hard time accepting what she had done.

Grandma Rose continued. "We have no idea if Lacey knew that Abby is the Chosen One or if she chose Abby randomly." This seemed to satisfy the crowd for the moment.

"I should explain something to the new recruits," Grandma Rose continued. "As I've already said, unicorn blood has healing powers. The Drenykin capture and imprison unicorns because they administer the sacred blood to their wounded and sick warriors.

"What might interest you to understand, is when the blood of a unicorn gets into a recipient's veins, the unicorn becomes a small piece of that person. Furthermore, those who receive the sacred blood become hopelessly devoted to the unicorn whose blood they share.

"As you can imagine, when the Elders became aware of Lacey Lynn's fate, we held some small hope that Lacey's blood running in Drenykin veins might soften some of them to our ways. But there is no way to know if that might happen and it is only conjecture.

"What cannot be ignored is that Lacey Lynn has paid a hard price for being a unicorn. And her loved ones have suffered along with her. Including me. Because Lacey Lynn is also my granddaughter."

"My sister," Teej mumbled under his breath. It was seriously past time she was back in the arms of her family.

"In the wee morning hours, you all heard the return of Abby's younger brother, Jack," Grandma went on. "Jack kept us busy putting out fires for several hours, didn't he? Well Jack, and several other family members wishing to save both Lacey and Abby, descended on the house where Lacey is imprisoned. To put a long story short, they ran into trouble. There were two casualties.

"Samantha Sider is already a legend among us for being born out of fire. She lost her arm in last night's battle. Fortunately, it has almost completely regenerated and she is battle-ready.

"Michael Bagwell, on the other hand, suffered a boating accident. He is alive but unconscious. Let us all pray that he will recover.

"Two of our warriors were captured. One of them is Rik Sider. The other is Cash McAllister, Abby's Appointed Protector. One warrior is missing in action. It is Travis Ryked, Lacey's only child.

"As you can see, it was truly a family affair," Rose said dryly. There was a small rumble of laughter in the crowd. *Yeah, yeah,* thought Teej. *Like you all wouldn't have done the same.*

It was his turn to speak. He didn't waste his time defending his family members. He briefly outlined Rik's original plan and how he likely came to be captured.

Next Torrents shared some of the other details, like Travis' powers as an empath. "His abilities are astonishing," Torrents bragged about his grandson. "I watched from my hiding place as he turned into the biggest, meanest, hell mongrel I've ever seen. In the first few minutes of setting foot on the property, he ripped out the throat of the pack leader guarding the land. Unfortunately, that's as far as I know. Whether his true identity has been discovered or not, I cannot say."

"But how do you know Rik and Cash were captured?" asked Cookies the Sprite. Teej was just getting to that part.

"Abby has seen Rik and Cash through Lacey's eyes. They are guarded by several hounds. Their commander is none other than our old friend, Jerematicus ..." Teej spit into the fire to show his distaste for the name "... Jones."

"Do the Drenykin know we're coming?" asked Lyll.

Grandma Rose spoke now. "We don't know the answer to that. But we will assume that they do." She turned to Abby and nodded at her.

Abby stepped forward confidently. She spoke loud and clear. "On this night, I call you to arms. Join me in this mission. Let it be the first of many successful battles under my reign as Chosen One."

She said it just like she had practiced, but the effect was much more devastating. "To arms," the warriors responded, raising their fists in unison. As they raised a battle cry, Teej flexed his arms and shrugged his shoulders restlessly. Abby was looking at him. He winked reassuringly at her before leaping into the air. Mid-leap, he phased into his gargoyle form and circled up into the sky.

Teej had no need to listen to the rest of the strategy briefing. He already knew the plan. There was no plan. They were going to show up en masse and take back what was theirs. They should have done this in the first place.

As he prepared himself mentally for the coming battle, he thanked the Creator for all his blessings, including the addition of a dragon to their ranks. With Jack and Duke on either side of him, nothing and no one could stop them. Teej was sure of it.

Julea

When she returned to her bedroom after the Fire, Julea almost fainted at the sight. In the center of the bed where Michael had lain was a large, black, smouldering hole in the mattress. "Oh my Goddess, Michael!" she cried. She heard footsteps behind her. It was her stepfather, Thom.

"Julea…" he said as he entered the room. He stopped when he saw the destruction.

"I shouldn't have left him," Julea sobbed. Maybe if she'd been there, she could have put out the flames.

"Shhhh," Thom said, strangely. He cocked his head to the side for a moment, and spoke quietly. "I've heard legends but never seen it with my own eyes," he said.

"What are you talking about?" Julea asked. Her stepfather's demeanour comforted her. He would not be so calm if he believed Michael to be dead.

"When a Phoenix rises, he is born in a burst of flames leaving a circle of burnt ashes behind," Thom replied softly. "My father told me that a newborn Phoenix hides nearby while he regains his strength."

As soon as he said it, Julea became aware of another presence in the room. She edged slowly towards the dark shadows of the walk-in closet. As she peered in, she heard a gasp. "Michael?" she said softly. He did not answer.

Julea's eyes adjusted to the darkness and she saw him. Huddled naked behind clothes and shoes, he sat shivering with his wings wrapped protectively around him. This was unlike any Phoenix Julea had ever seen. The Phoenix was usually a large bird, with brightly coloured tail feathers and an imposingly pointed beak. What huddled in the corner of her closet was part man and part bird. Julea was sure she had never seen anything so beautiful in her life.

Michael looked up at her imploringly. "What is happening to me, Julea?" he asked.

"I'm not sure," she replied hesitantly. "I shared my blood with you. I brought you back to life. But I did not know this would happen. I ... I suppose my blood has infused you with powers ..." She held her arms out to him.

"Be careful," Michael warned her. His feathers were still hot. He slowly rose to his feet and unfolded his wings uncertainly. He looked so vulnerable and fragile. Julea instinctively stepped into his arms embracing his trembling body. She had hugged her husband a thousand times, but it had never felt like this. He enfolded them both in his wings and lifted her effortlessly up to his face.

"I love you, Julea," he said. Then his lips were upon hers. She felt so much love in his kiss. For the first time in her entire life, Julea felt utterly safe.

Travis

It was much easier than he thought it would be to convince a few pack members to join his traitorous mission. He persuaded them that the "house pets" were getting the best food and the best positions, yet they were slovenly and fat. They would make easy targets, he reasoned. He needn't have tried so hard to convince them. It was their pleasure to join him.

One-by-one, they took them out. Each time a hound from Jerematicus' personal guard wandered away from the house to urinate or stretch his legs; his destiny was assured. A quick and quiet death.

The others wanted to prolong the killing process but Travis was adamant. "We can do a lot more damage if they don't see or hear what we're doing," he quipped derisively.

The other hounds sneered companionably. "Yes," they agreed. "We'll take them one-by-one before they even realize it's happening." Years of built-up hatred for Jerematicus' spoiled, personal guard culminated in a fury of ripping and tearing. Afterwards, they would change into their natural forms to clean up the mess.

Travis was surprised to see how normal they looked in their human forms. He wondered how many times he'd passed a Drenykin hound on the street.

As Jerematicus' personal guard diminished, Travis was amused to find they weren't missed. In a matter of hours, six Drenykin house hounds were terminated. General morale among Travis' own pack members was high. They were enjoying themselves.

Once Jerematicus himself appeared on the porch asking where a particular guard was. The other hounds grunted sleepily from their lounging positions. They didn't know. They didn't care.

Travis paced the edge of the forest surrounding the house looking for opportunities to weaken the enemy.

Could he somehow convince his pack to help him rescue his mother? He seriously doubted it. He'd stick with his first plan. Become one of his mother's guards.

Cash

Hearing Abby's voice had shaken him to the core. His fur stood on end constantly now, as he bristled with fear. Lacey was conscious now, but delirious. Cash hoped Abby was okay. Where was she? At least he knew she was alive.

The hellhounds in the room sensed his anxiety the way dogs do. Some of them grinned at him, tongues lolling, mocking him. Others found his incessant pacing nerve-wracking. They sent him glares and snarls. But Cash could no easier sit still than grow wings. Captivity was definitely not something he could get used to.

Perhaps it was this heightened state of alertness that made his hearing so sensitive. But Cash was sure he heard it first. It was the sound of redemption.

Julea

In the end, no one stayed behind except the McAllisters and some of the others who guarded the lands. As they lifted off into the sky, carrying their comrades, Julea felt his eyes on her. Michael had not left her side since she'd found him. While everyone else prepared for battle, Julea and Michael had spent time alone.

Julea told him everything that had happened since his boat capsized on Okanagan Lake. How he had arrived cold and dead. How she had nursed him through the night, dripping blood from her hand into his mouth. How

Abby had been dying before her eyes. And finally, how she had lost the baby. Their daughter.

Michael held her while they both cried. He consoled her lovingly. Julea had never felt so close to him. The Michael she'd grown to know over the years did not show a lot of love. Julea had never felt safe sharing herself completely with him. He had always been reserved emotionally. It was something Julea had learned to accept.

Now, with his arms wrapped around her and his voice caressing her, Julea was shattered. She hadn't realized how starved for affection she'd become until she was being enveloped by it. Her whole body and soul shivered in receipt of his love.

The day before, Julea was a different woman. Pregnant and impatient, she'd waited for her children and husband to return from a deadly mission. Tonight, she joined the battle with her husband flying beside her. She could never have predicted any of this.

Even as she felt Michael's loving and protective gaze on her, she felt the disapproving stares and glares of the others. It was no great effort to imagine how Michael, a mere human, had suddenly developed such incredible powers. A unicorn's blood was infinitely powerful. And Julea was a unicorn.

Her secret was no secret. Any shame that she felt was erased in the glow of Michael's adoration. Everything external fell away and what remained was only the two of them and their children. Tonight, they went to war for the children who lived. Tomorrow they would mourn the child they'd lost.

Travis

His murdering ways decreased the enemy's numbers but Travis didn't end up needing to find a way into the house. It was delivered by mass invasion. The family arrived.

First, they came from the sky: gargoyles with their menacing growls waving their stone tails; Jack swooping in, the size of a house, lighting up the night sky with flames every few seconds; faeries fluttered in looking so innocent and sweet, yet their faces bore grave intentions of violence.

Elves, centaurs, giants, and every other grounded creature you could imagine swarmed out of the trees into the light of the house. The lakefront came alive with supernatural creatures swimming among the waves. Water sprites hovered above the water to block off any escape by their enemy.

As the Fatum converged on the property from every direction, Travis took advantage of the chaos. Fighting erupted around him, but he had not lost sight of his goal. He meant to find his mother. He watched for a chance to get inside.

That chance arrived immediately. In his haste to get to the unguarded doorway, Travis forgot his disguise. To anyone who saw him, he was a hellhound! Travis was suddenly thrown sideways by what appeared to be a massive, rock man who towered over him. Before Travis could react, the rock man raised his fist to finish him off. Grandpa Torrents saved him.

"Stop!" he commanded the rock beast. "That's Travis. He's one of us."

"Oops, sorry Travis," the rock man said in a sweet, familiar, feminine voice. "I didn't recognize you."

"Aunt Sheena?" Travis asked tentatively.

"Yes, it's me, Darlin'. I'll watch your back while you go get your mom."

Travis was more than a little rattled to hear his beautiful aunt's sweet voice coming from the giant, scary, rock creature. But he collected himself and thanked her. He was through the door and in the house a moment later. Aunt Sheena followed as far as the door but because of her size, she couldn't follow him in.

Sneakily and silently, Travis headed for the rooms at the back of his house where, according to the house pets, they kept his mother. Jerematicus was in the first room Travis came to. The door was slightly ajar. Jerematicus had his back to Travis, speaking to one of his mutts. "Order the pack to hold them off while I escape with the Fatum healer. Kill the elf and the wolf," he said. Travis slunk past without being noticed.

In the hall, Travis caught the familiar scent of his cousin, Cash. He tracked it to the last door in the corridor. It was open a crack but Travis could not see in. He nudged the door with his nose and slipped inside the room.

The first thing he saw was Cash in his wolf form standing protectively over his mother's body. Around them, dead and near-dead hounds littered the floor. Cash looked up at Travis, opening his eyes first in recognition, then in horror.

"NOOOO!" Cash screamed inside his head, but a cold blade across his throat prevented Travis from understanding. Everything faded to black.

Rik

"Give him my blood," she begged. But there was no time to lose. They needed to escape. She must have read his mind. "He won't survive unless we do it now," Lacey Lynn pleaded.

Rik knew she was right. "What do you want me to do?" he asked. He looked around for a bag of blood before remembering that Jerematicus had taken them from the room when he spared their lives.

"It must be fresh from my body, Rik." Lacey explained gently. "Open my palm with your blade."

Rik looked down at the blade he'd used moments before to kill every hound in the room. If Cash hadn't howled so loudly, Travis would be dead too. He pulled a lighter out of his pocket and hastily sterilized the knife. He held it out to Lacey.

"No, you must do it," she begged. "I am too weak."

"Why are people always asking me to hurt them?" the tattoo artist replied.

Normally a slice across the palm of a unicorn was nothing to be concerned about. Her own blood would heal the wound quickly and seamlessly. But Lacey was very weak. She had already lost too much blood. Rik feared she would die for such a gash in her hand.

"He is my son," Lacey said. In the moment when Rik had sliced his throat, Travis resumed his human form. He lay bleeding at Rik's feet, unconscious and turning blue.

Rik was decisive. He grasped Lacey's hand, made a smooth incision across her palm and held her hand over Travis's slit throat.

Her arm went limp. She'd fainted. Rik thanked the Creator for that blessing at least. The hardest people to hurt were the women in his life. They were also the people he hurt the most.

Three years of being bled a little at a time had weakened Lacey's body but it had not weakened her blood. In mere moments, Travis' wound reformed into unbroken skin and he regained consciousness, gasping and sitting upright suddenly. Rik wrapped Lacey's hand while Travis got his bearings. Her hand wasn't healing so fast.

The entire ordeal lasted about five minutes but it was too late for them to escape. The door swung in to reveal Jerematicus, dressed to travel in a black leather jacket and gloves. He stopped short, taking in the dead bodies of his personal guard. For a brief moment, Jerematicus forgot his emotional shield and grief flickered in his eyes. He mastered his expression quickly.

"Well, I guess I underestimated you," Jerematicus said, his voice calm and light. "I came to fetch the prisoner." He held out his hand as though he expected Rik to hand her over.

Rik held her tight hoping it would prevent Jerematicus from using a force field to separate them. Cash bared his teeth viciously, blocking Jerematicus' path to Lacey and Rik.

Jerematicus looked bored. He flicked his hand towards Cash, as though he was swatting away a mosquito. Rik had seen those hand movements before. He flinched expecting to see Cash go flying across the room. But nothing happened. Rik wasn't the only one shocked. An expression of fear spread across Jerematicus' face.

"What's this?" Jerematicus demanded. He stared curiously at Cash, scrunched his eyebrows with determination, and raised his hand as if to smack Cash on the head. Again, Rik flinched expecting Cash to be flattened before his eyes. But the force that Jerematicus sent out bounced back instead. It sent Jerematicus flying into the wall behind him.

Rik watched as his nemesis picked himself off the ground, shaking his head. "How?" he asked, staring into Rik's eyes. But it wasn't Rik who answered him. From beside him, Travis' voice nearly hissed with contempt.

"I'd advise you to leave my mother alone now," he said menacingly. Jerematicus jerked his eyes towards Travis.

"That was you?"

"Would you like to find out what else I am capable of?" Travis replied sweetly.

Jerematicus was no fool. Rik had to acknowledge that the man was not only powerful but intelligent. He seemed to realize his predicament.

"Ahh, I see," he said. "You're an empath. You can match anything I can conjure."

"Why don't we test that theory?" Travis offered. Rik was a bit taken back by his nephew's ferocity. He sure was cocky for a new recruit.

Jerematicus laughed. "I don't need to test anything, child," he replied. "You see, someone very close to me is also an empath. I am well aware of the degree of your derangement." It was an odd thing to say. Rik knew it meant something personal, but he couldn't imagine what.

Jerematicus looked regretfully at Lacey for a moment before chuckling softly. "I will be off then." He turned on his heels and left the room.

They were silent for a moment, listening to the sounds of battle being waged outside the walls. Rik was stunned that Jerematicus had not put up more of a fight. Cash looked at Rik briefly before running out the door. Travis held his arms out for his mother.

It was difficult to do, but Rik let go of his sister and handed her limp body to her son. "Let's go home," he said kindly to his nephew.

Jack

Uncle Duke took the front door and Jack took the back door, their great dragon wings snapping as they hovered in the sky above the house. Uncle Teej flew around them in a figure eight, his huge stone gargoyle tail whipping around him with fury as he watched for his prey. The three of them had made a pact. Jerematicus would not survive the night.

Chaos raged around them. Fatum warriors faced off with Drenykin warriors and hounds. Cries, snarls, and growls filled the air. Abby had insisted on being a part of the ground action. Jack knew she was looking for Cash.

He looked down at his sister. She walked confidently through the melee with their mother and father on either side.

Jack became momentarily mesmerized by his mother who walked purposefully beside Abby in her unicorn form. Her horn was covered in blood. Her wings were tucked back as she pranced and snorted menacingly.

To Jack's horror, Abby suddenly fell to the ground. No one had touched her. Jack was confused. He watched as his father picked Abby up into his arms and enfolded her in his wings.

Jack's mother let out an ear-piercing sound, like nothing he'd ever heard before. She kicked her front legs up, lowering her horn dangerously for anyone who came near Michael and Abby.

"Jack!" Uncle Teej growled mildly as he swooped past Jack. "Pay attention!" Just then, a flying creature flew at him hissing. She was stunningly beautiful. A woman with wings. And fangs. Despite her incredible beauty, she had a horrible odour. Jack shuddered. He bathed her in a shower of flames.

The creature quickly protected herself with a shield. Similar, smaller, flying creatures surrounded him. A giant flap of his wing sent most of them tumbling through the air. But the beautiful, flying woman was back. She brandished a shiny blade in one hand and a tarnished shield in the other. Jack knew she would go for his throat. There was one soft spot on a dragon that could be pierced by a

blade. You had to get near it first. The harpy was determined to try.

Again, Jack bathed the darting damsel in fire. Again,
she shielded herself, although Jack could smell burnt
feathers. She was gearing up for another offensive move
when she was suddenly plucked out of the sky by powerful talons. "Stop playing around with harpies, Jack," Uncle
Teej said as he carried off the screaming creature. Jack
wondered if he was joking.

He looked down at the house below him and the
back door he was guarding. To his surprise, at that very
moment, a man stepped out of the door. The man was
hauntingly familiar. Jack would never forget that face.
He had met this man in Principal Logan's office several
months before. It was Jeremy Jones' father.

"That's him!" Teej roared as he flung the flailing harpy
in the lake. He came flying back towards Jack. "Get him
before he makes the change!"

Jack descended forcefully towards Jerematicus Jones
but everything seemed to happen in slow motion. Mr.
Jones stepped off the porch into mid-air and began to
change form. Pitch-black wings sprouted and folded out
from his shoulder blades. The moonlight made his white
hair glow like a flame.

Jack watched as his target rose quickly into the sky.
He had been briefed thoroughly regarding Jerematicus'
powers. He was a shape-shifter faery with the power to
create force fields.

"Move it, fledgling." Mr. Jones' voice was mocking as
he approached Jack. He looked like an avenging angel in

this form, with penetrating red eyes and blood-red lips. While noticing these things, Jack suddenly felt an invisible force slamming into him. He went sprawling through the air, scrambling for balance.

Teej flew swiftly and silently towards Jerematicus, but the evil faerie, without even looking, merely waved a hand in his direction. Some kind of invisible force bounced off Teej knocking him out of the sky. Jack watched his uncle fall, like a ton of bricks, to the ground. Grandpa Torrents descended immediately to protect him.

As Jack recovered himself, Uncle Duke attempted to torch Jerematicus from behind. Again, Jerematicus waved his hand flippantly, creating an invisible force field that prevented the flames from reaching him and almost knocked Uncle Duke out of the sky. Duke flapped his dragon wings violently, trying not to fall.

"You see, Jack Sider?" Mr. Jones said as he stared penetratingly into Jack's eyes. "I knew we should meet again. Too bad you're an infant and no match for me." Mr. Jones chuckled derisively. If there was one thing Jack could not stand, it was being treated like a child. Smoke poured out of his nostrils as he struggled to control his temper.

Jerematicus laughed again. "Oh Jack, do give your grandmother my best if you make it out alive." He turned his back to fly away. Jack had to do something.

At that moment, Grandma Dianna appeared before Jerematicus. Jack found it difficult to see her but her voice was loud and clear. "I cannot allow you to leave, JJ" she said.

"Hello Dianna," Jerematicus greeted her. "We were just talking about you … It's a little late to rekindle old passions," he sneered, opening his arms and shrugging his shoulders. They hovered in the air facing each other, their wings fluttering effortlessly — Jerematicus' large, imposing faery form dwarfing Grandma Dianna's tiny little pixie form.

"There was a time when I held you in high regard, JJ," she replied. "I would never have pegged you for a Drenykin turncoat. Then."

"Yes, well, you never really knew me," Jerematicus said. He smiled. "Now dear, I really must be going."

As his grandmother spoke to Mr. Jones, Jack descended quietly from behind. The battle cries around them muffled the snapping of his wings. But Jerematicus seemed oblivious to Jack's approach anyway. He had his full attention on Grandma Dianna.

"I would apologize, JJ, but I'm not sorry," Grandma Dianna persisted. "You're not going anywhere."

"And who is going to stop me?" Jerematicus scoffed. "None of you have even a fraction of the power I have. Your empath is otherwise occupied. And you'll have to kill me to stop me."

Jerematicus continued his ascent, laughing down at Grandma Dianna as he went. He didn't realize he was flying right into Jack's reach. At such close range, Jack did the first thing that came naturally. He seized the dark faerie in his claws and promptly bit off his head.

Grandma Dianna lowered her face regretfully before getting in the last word. "If you insist," she replied gravely.

Julea

Goddess, it was good to be home. Her children were safe and alive. Her sister was returned and reunited with her family. Abby and Lacey were still weak but they'd revived during the flight back. Julea knew they would both recover.

Lacey was barely reunited with her loved ones before being whisked off to appear before the Elders. She'd already told Julea the whole story.

"I was disoriented and lost, in and out of consciousness," Lacey explained. "One minute I was floating on a cloud through space, the next I was coughing up blood. On some level, I knew I was going to die. I reached out with my heart and begged our Creator for mercy. In the next moment, there was a flash of light in the void. At least that was what it felt like. I heard…or maybe I felt…a powerful force growing. I seized the chance to connect with someone, anyone, before I died. She was the only light on the horizon."

"Did you know she was the Chosen One?" Julea asked.

"All I knew was that she was the Chosen One."

"What do you mean?"

"I mean…I didn't know she was your daughter…my niece," Lacey whispered, her voice full of regret. "I didn't know she was our last hope for salvation either."

"I knew you had a good reason," Julea responded quietly.

"I'm so sorry, Julea." Lacey's voice squeaked as she broke into tears.

"Hey, I'm just glad my baby sister is back home where she belongs." Julea said soothingly. As they embraced,

Julea quickly counted her blessings. Think of the ones who survived, she told herself.

Now as she lay alone on her bed, she sighed heavily. This was the first time since Jack returned with his dead father's body that Julea was alone.

She tried not to think about the baby. It was difficult because she'd been feeling painful contractions for several hours. Even though she wanted it to be over, she dreaded the part where she would miscarry the baby. Seeing her daughter's small, lifeless body would be too much after everything else.

She focused on breathing as another contraction seized her. When her muscles released, she found herself crying. The tears came like a flood. And so, it went. Contraction. Tears. Contraction. Tears. About twenty minutes into it, Michael entered the room.

"Julea," he said. "Are you awake?"

"Yes," she whispered.

"What's wrong?" he asked as he came to her side. He brushed her hair off her forehead and noticed she was sweating. "What's going on?" he demanded worriedly.

"I'm having a miscarriage," she said. She concentrated on keeping her hands relaxed as she breathed through another contraction. The pain was too great now for tears.

Michael called out the door. "Dianna, come quick. Please hurry!"

Julea started to feel her body pushing the fetus out. She tried to hold back until some towels had been placed underneath her, but she could feel the baby coming. She didn't know a miscarriage could be so debilitating.

This was like full-term labour, yet she'd only been four months pregnant.

"She's coming," Julea heard her mother say. The mood in the room was sombre as they waited for the corpse to come out. Julea took a deep breath and pushed hard on the next contraction. She wanted it to be over. Now.

"Here she comes," Dianna said. "She's … she's … she's moving!" Despite her disorientation, Julea's heart nearly burst at the news. She was premature, but Julea was a healer. Her blood was more powerful than any doctor or hospital in the world. If her baby was alive, Julea could keep her that way.

Michael now stood at her feet, watching the birth of their very much alive little girl. "She's tiny, but she's turning her head and scrunching her eyes," he reported to Julea as their daughter was handed to him.

"But I don't understand," Julea sniffed. Her tears flowed again. Michael placed the tiny infant on Julea's stomach and covered her with a face cloth. Julea held her close in the palm of her hand. "I couldn't feel her anymore. My compulsion to fight had returned…"

As Julea stammered confusedly, Dianna pulled back the cloth and began to wash the blood off the infant. Suddenly she screamed and jumped back. Emotionally preparing herself for the worst, Julea cupped the newborn in her hands and lifted her up to see what had scared her mother. Laid flat and wet against her tiny body at each shoulder blade were little bent wing nubs and folded against each side of her head, pointed ears.

"No wonder you couldn't feel anything," Dianna exclaimed. "She's an elf!"

Abby

She laid in the grass with her hair spread out around her, letting the breeze caress her face. Beside her, lying on his side, Cash lazily tickled her arm with the petals of a cuckoo flower.

Their reunion was bittersweet. She awoke in his arms on the back of a dragon and realized it wasn't rain she'd felt, but tears. Cash held her close while they rode between Jack's scaly shoulder blades. Later he admitted he'd been praying. "The Creator answers prayers," he said.

Now they lounged. It occurred to Abby that this is what teenagers do. Lounge around, hang out with their friends, go shopping, fall in love … Teenagers don't normally turn into mermaids and go to war. Human teenagers, at least. She had always known she was different from most people she met. She just never imagined that it was because she was only part human.

"Don't ever leave me again," Cash said again. She was surprised to see how he'd suffered. The colour was coming back into his cheeks now. Grandma Rose said they were connected and should never be apart.

"That was Rik's first mistake," Grandma Rose complained in retrospect. "He should never have taken her away from her Appointed Protector!"

Abby didn't bother reminding Grandma Rose that the real danger came from Lacey's enchantment. She'd been in danger at the farm, with Cash by her side. She just hadn't known it yet.

"Promise?" Cash teased.

"I promise." Abby meant it with all her heart. She twisted her hands in the front of Cash's shirt and pulled him in for a kiss. They remained motionless after the kiss ended, cheek-to-cheek. Abby breathed in his scent, relishing the heat coming off his skin.

The sound of throat clearing made them jump. It was Michael carrying a little bundle in his hands. Abby's new baby sister. She couldn't help squealing as she jumped up to see little Josie.

"She's sleeping," said Michael as he shielded her face from the sun. He sat down in the grass beside Cash.

"Can I hold her?" Abby pleaded.

"Sure, but she's so tiny and new ... can you sit down while you hold her?" Michael asked.

"Yes. Yes, I can," Abby agreed eagerly. She plopped down on Michael's other side. He explained how to hold Josie as he handed her over.

"We have to be careful of her wing buds," he said. "We want them nice and healthy for her little wings to grow."

Abby was truly amazed at the change in Michael since his resurrection. He literally glowed with happiness and love. Such a change from the quiet, angry tyrant she was used to. He looked the same in most ways except his larger size. Abby found she was getting used to the wings.

"Aren't you going to turn them off?" Abby asked, staring unabashedly at Michael's wings. Even baby Josie changed back and forth between her forms from one moment to the next. Why was Michael still walking around with wings?

Michael laughed. "I've been trying but I can't seem to figure it out," he replied. "Maybe mine are permanent."

"That would be weird," Abby said. They both laughed.

"So, why did Josie get her powers already?" Abby asked Michael. She'd been waiting for someone to explain it to her. "Why doesn't she have to wait until she's fourteen like the rest of us?"

"Well, your Grandma Rose says that it is very rare but sometimes a Fatum fetus develops powers in the womb. Usually after it has suffered some kind of trauma. The theory is that Josie felt threatened in the womb, so she developed her powers spontaneously to protect herself."

"But why couldn't Mom feel her moving?"

"I'm not an expert on elves, but I am told that they are very good at hiding. Josie was playing a trick on your mother." Michael's silly grin was contagious.

"She was probably hiding instinctively," Cash suggested.

Michael nodded. "I guess a wolf would know something about instincts," he replied as he looked at Cash.

"Yeah, um, speaking of that, Sir," said Cash. "I want to apologize for my deception. You said I was not allowed on the property, and yet I came in disguise like a coward. I am ashamed of myself."

"I understand a little better now about the two of you," Michael acknowledged. "Being apart isn't really an option. It's the same for Julea and I, now that her blood runs in my veins," he said seriously. "To be honest, I'm not really that angry guy you knew me as anymore. Even my name,

'Michael,' sounds wrong when I hear it. I feel like I am not Michael anymore." He stared into the distance for a moment before realizing that Abby was waiting for something. "Oh, and I forgive you both," he said smiling.

"Oh, thank you, Michael," Abby cried. If her hands weren't full of baby elf, she would wrap her stepfather in a giant hug. She had dreaded this conversation. "I am so relieved." She looked back down at the small baby cupped in her hands.

"Why is she so little?" she asked.

"Well, for one thing, Josie is premature. Your mother was only four months pregnant when Josie got her powers. When she made the change, she became capable of living outside of the womb. She'll be the size of most newborns in about five months."

"Wow," said Abby. "How do you know? What if she stays tiny?"

"That's what I said. But your Grandma Rose said look at Kade! He's growing just fine!" Michael emphasized his words to sound like Grandma on a rant. Abby giggled.

"Kade got his powers in the womb too?"

"Yes, his mother was wounded right before she became pregnant. Her belly grew and her bruises didn't fade fast enough. A neighbour alerted the Ministry thinking she was being abused. They apprehended Kade shortly after his birth. It didn't help that he kept disappearing. The social workers would show up and his mother would be frantically trying to find him. It didn't look too good."

"What is his power?" Cash asked curiously.

"He's a faerie with the ability to make himself invisible. Kade kept disappearing on his foster parents too. Eventually they ran out of families willing to take him and gave him back to his parents. Now, his parents are keeping him on sacred land until he learns to control his powers. We'll have to do the same thing with Josie."

Abby looked down at her. Now, she looked completely human. Her wing nubs had disappeared and her eyes appeared less angular. "She even changes form in her sleep!" Abby was amazed.

"I know. It's crazy, isn't it?" Michael couldn't stop staring at Josie. "Apparently Kade did the same thing. People would go to check on him, and he would be gone. But of course, he wasn't gone. He was just invisible."

Abby felt a small pang of jealousy to see Michael so happy and in love with baby Josie. She wondered if Michael had ever looked at her the same way when she was a baby.

"Well, I should get Josie back to your mother. She gets anxious if I take too long," Michael said as he carefully scooped Josie out of Abby's hands. He leaned over and kissed Abby on the forehead. "I love you and I'm happy to see you happy."

"Uh, thank you," Abby said. For some reason, tears threatened to spill. She held them in, took a deep breath, then sprawled on her stomach as she watched Michael walk back towards the house.

"Are you okay?" Cash asked. She turned to look at him. His beautiful face. His wavy hair. His muscular arms.

Gosh, how she loved him. She moved into his arms and put her face against his chest.

"Everything is amazing," she said.

Jack

"There's one thing I don't understand," Jack told his Uncle Duke. They sat at a table out of the way, so they could hear each other over the music. People swarmed the dance floor. It was the biggest event of the year in Beaverdell. The Sider Costume Ball. "Why do you have to have your powers before you receive The Knowledge?"

Duke had taken Jack under his wing. In this case, it was literal. He'd been teaching Jack how to get the most out of his powers. Two dragons, sometimes three when Travis decided to join them, circling the sky over the Sider homestead, spitting fire occasionally. Just another day in the life of Jack Bagwell.

"Well, clearly we can't have a bunch of children burdened with The Knowledge. They deserve a childhood. And once they're older, well, most of them wouldn't believe it anyway," Duke replied.

"Bring them to the reunion," Jack suggested. "Seeing is believing. It would have been a lot easier for my family to get me to eat an apple, if they had told me I'd get powers," insisted Jack.

"As you know, what we call a Fatum child right before he or she makes the change, is a Green Tree. That's why your Uncle Rik was making fun of you. It probably seems childish, but it's part of our tradition to make fun of the Green Trees."

Jack laughed. Next year would be his turn to make fun of Green Trees.

"We've tried passing on The Knowledge to Green Trees before. The results are always the same. They take forever to make the change. It seems like knowing that it's going to happen interferes with the process in some way. Then you have Green Trees taking part in the strategy meetings and feeling the pull to join The Cause..." Duke shook his head pointedly. "It's not meant to be."

"Does everything have to do with destiny?" asked Jack. "Is nothing left to chance?"

"I don't know," Duke replied honestly. "Take that tree of yours, for instance. Has anyone told you about the mirage?"

"No," Jack said.

"Well, weren't you surprised when you suddenly found a massively tall tree in the middle of the orchard that you'd never seen before?"

"Uh, yes," replied Jack. "I wondered how I'd missed it."

"Yeah, well, you made that tree."

"No, I didn't," Jack said defensively. "I didn't even have powers yet."

"You didn't have powers but you made that tree. There's an enchantment on the Sider land called a Great Desire Mirage. No one knows when or if they will step through the mirage, but when they do, whatever is their greatest desire will manifest."

"My greatest desire was a massive, climbing tree?" Jack asked incredulously.

Duke laughed. "Apparently, it was."

"Thank Goddess it wasn't something more dangerous, like a…girlfriend," Jack joked.

"You're reading my mind, man," Duke replied. "We've all sat around talking about the what ifs of someone wandering into the mirage with an embarrassing or deadly great desire. But it's never happened. Every time someone actually does wander into the mischievous enchantment, his great desire is something simple and glorious. Like a massive, climbing tree."

"So, you're saying that destiny controls who wanders into the Great Desire Mirage?"

"I'm not saying anything at all," Duke assured him. "I'm saying I don't know."

They laughed as Grandpa Torrents arrived at their table. "Hey there, Buds," he said to Jack. "Can I have a word?" Uncle Duke stood up to leave, but Torrents stopped him. "You can stay, Duke," he said. They sat down.

Grandpa Torrents was dressed like an eagle. The costume was magnificent, although not as magnificent as the real thing. He must have noticed Jack staring. "These are all my own feathers," he said proudly. "I collected them purposefully for this costume."

"It's a great costume," Jack said, with sincere admiration.

"So, here's the thing I wanted to talk to you about." Although no one could have heard them over the music, Grandpa Torrents leaned in confidentially. "You're a hero in our family now. You killed a man who is not only our enemy because he is a Drenykin, but because he has taken great pleasure in torturing our own family members."

"Is he the one who tortured Uncle Rik?" Jack asked.

"Yes," Grandpa Torrents replied. Duke nodded his head. "We are all very grateful for what you've done and you've certainly earned bragging rights. But I want you to take it easy telling the story around the reunion."

"Okay," agreed Jack. "I wasn't planning on boasting about it," he said. Truthfully, he couldn't wait to tell all his cousins about it and anyone else who would listen. "May I ask why, Grandpa T?"

"I want you to keep this next information private. Duke already knows about this. It's nobody's business but your grandmother's and the late Jerematicus Jones, but there was a time before Dianna and I met that Jerematicus was courting her."

Jack didn't hide his surprise. "But, he's a Drenykin!"

"He wasn't always a Drenykin," Duke supplied. "He used to be one of us. One of our most powerful warriors."

"You mean you can choose?"

"Well certainly," Grandpa Torrents replied. "You are born into one camp or the other, but the Creator gave us all free will. Some of us even go among humans and stay straight for a while. Like your mom did while you were growing up."

"So, he changed sides?" Jack was shocked. Why would someone choose to be the bad guy?

"That's right," said Torrents. "Jerematicus was a Drenykin sympathizer. I think maybe he stayed Fatum as long as he did because he was in love with your grandmother." Things started to fall into place for Jack. The way Mr. Jones had treated him the first time they met in the principal's office. How he hissed the Sider name when he spoke it. How Grandma Dianna had intercepted him as he was making his escape. He was so distracted by her that it gave Jack an opportunity no one in the family had ever had before. The opportunity to bite off his head."

Jack cringed remembering the foul taste. "So, what happened? Grandma didn't love him back?"

"She tried. Then she met me. Even though Jerematicus, or JJ as she called him, was far more powerful than I was, she chose me. She said it was because I was a good dancer." Grandpa Torrents looked downcast for a moment. "I can't say I deserved the honour, but I did my best."

"So, Jerematicus turned Drenykin and made a special effort to hurt Grandma Dianna's children?" Jack already didn't like the guy, but this was too much. "No wonder he was a turncoat. His soul was black."

"Yes, it was," Uncle Duke agreed. "But he was a smart, funny guy if you caught him on a good day." They laughed.

"So, you don't want me to talk about killing Jerematicus because he used to date Grandma Dianna?" Jack was still confused.

"I think it would be the respectful thing to do. Your grandmother has always felt responsible for the horrible things Jerematicus did to our children. For all of your safety but also for her own sanity, she had a stake in putting an end to his tyranny more than any of us. For many years, every time she heard his name, your Grandma felt terrible guilt for the pain he has caused our family. Spare your old Grandma's feelings and make sure she's not around when you talk about it. Alright, Buds?"

"Sure. Of course," replied Jack. Grandpa Torrents thanked him, then made his way to the dance floor. Jack turned back to his Uncle Duke. "He acts like he's still married to her," he remarked of his Grandfather's consideration for Grandma Dianna's feelings.

"I think he probably feels bad because he wasn't a very good husband," Duke answered. "Maybe it's his way of making up for it a little. He obviously still loves her."

"Yeah, you're probably right," said Jack. "People sure do a lot of crazy things for love."

"Love is the only good reason to do anything," Duke replied wisely.

Jack nodded. He'd never been in love before. He looked over at the crowded dance floor. There were several girls his age laughing and dancing. One of them looked his way. For a moment, their eyes met. The girl blushed and turned away quickly.

"Well, that's my cue," Jack said, rising out of his seat.

"You off to find love?" Duke asked.

"Nah, I'm just going to dance," Jack replied.